Frederic William Henry Myers

Essays

Classical

Frederic William Henry Myers

Essays
Classical

ISBN/EAN: 9783337177898

Hergestellt in Europa, USA, Kanada, Australien, Japan

Cover: Foto ©Andreas Hilbeck / pixelio.de

Weitere Bücher finden Sie auf **www.hansebooks.com**

ESSAYS

CLASSICAL

BY

F. W. H. MYERS

𝔏𝔬𝔫𝔡𝔬𝔫

MACMILLAN AND CO., Limited

NEW YORK: THE MACMILLAN COMPANY

1897

CONTENTS.

PREFATORY NOTE.

IN reprinting this Essay from *Hellenica*, I have thought it needless to repeat my original list of authorities consulted. Since the Essay was written M. Bouché-Leclercq has published his *Histoire de la Divination dans l'Antiquité*, where the bibliography of the subject is given with exhaustive fulness. The chief resources to oracles in classical authors have been long ago collected, and are now the common property of scholars. The last considerable addition to the list was made by G. Wolff, and they have been judiciously arranged by Maury and others. What is needed is a true comprehension of them, towards which less progress has been made than the ordinary reader may suppose. Even Bouché-Leclercq, whose accuracy and completeness within his self-proposed limits deserve high admiration, expressly excludes from his purview the lessons and methods of comparative ethnology, and hardly cares to consider what those phenomena in reality *were* whose history he is recounting. I can claim little more of insight into their true nature than suffices to make me conscious of ignorance, but I have at least tried to indicate where the problems lie, and in what general directions we must look for their solution.

It is indeed true (as was remarked by several critics when this Essay first appeared) that I have kept but inadequately my implied promise of illustrating ancient mysteries by the light of modern discovery. But my difficulty lay not in the defect but in the excess of parallelism between ancient and modern phenomena. I found that each explicit reference of this kind would raise so many questions that the sequence of the narrative would soon have been destroyed. I was obliged, therefore, to content myself with suggestions and allusions — allusions necessarily obscure to the general reader in the absence of any satisfactory treatise on similar phenomena to which he could be referred. I am not without hope that this blank may before long be filled up by a research conducted on a wider and sounder basis than heretofore; and, should the sway of recognised law extend itself farther over that shadowy land, I shall be well content if this Essay

shall be thought to have aimed, however imperfectly, at that "true interrogation" which is "the
half of science."

POSTSCRIPT, 1887.

Since the above words were written in 1883,
some beginning of the suggested inquiries has been
recorded in the *Proceedings* of the Society for
Psychical Research. Some discussions on human
automatism which will there be found are not
without bearing on the subject of the present essay.

POSTSCRIPT, 1897.

The work of the Society for Psychical Research
has now been pushed much further; and its
Proceedings (Kegan Paul, Trench, Trübner & Co.)
are indispensable for persons interested in the
inquiries above referred to.

GREEK ORACLES.

Οὐ μέν πως νῦν ἔστιν ἀπὸ δρυὸς οὐδ' ἀπὸ πέτρης
τῷ ὀαριζέμεναι, ἅ τε παρθένος ἠΐθεός τε,
παρθένος ἠΐθεός τ' ὀαρίζετον ἀλλήλοιιν.

I.

IT is not only in the domain of physical inquiry
that the advance of knowledge is self-accelerated at
every step, and the very excellence of any given
work insures its own speedier supersession. All
those studies which bear upon the past of mankind
are every year more fully satisfying this test of the
genuinely scientific character of the plan on which
they are pursued. The old conception of the world's
history as a collection of stories, each admitting of
a complete and definitive recital, is giving way to
a conception which would compare it rather with
a series of imperfectly-read inscriptions, the sense
of each of which is modified by the interpretations
which we gradually find for its predecessors.

And of no department is this truer than of the
comparative history of religions. The very idea of

such a study is of recent growth, and no sooner is the attempt made to colligate by general laws the enormous mass of the religious phenomena of the world than we find that the growing science is in danger of being choked by its own luxuriance—that each conflicting hypothesis in turn seems to draw superabundant proof from the myriad beliefs and practices of men. We may, indeed, smile at the extravagances of one-sided upholders of each successive system. We need not believe with Bishop Huet[1] that Moses was the archetype both of Adonis and of Priapus. Nor, on the other hand, need we suppose with Pierson[2] that Abraham himself was originally a stone god. We may leave Dozy[3] to pursue his own conjecture, and deduce the strange story of the Hebrew race from their worship of the planet Saturn. Nor need the authority of Anonymus *de Rebus Incredibilibus*[4] constrain us to accept his view that Paris was a young man who wrote essays on goddesses, and Phaethon an unsuccessful astronomer.

But it is far from easy to determine the relative validity of the theories of which these are exaggerated expressions,—to decide (for instance) what place is to be given to the direct transference of

---

[1] *Demonstr. Evang.* iii. 3, viii. 5.
[2] Ap. Kuenen, *Religion of Israel*, i. 390.
[3] *Ibid.* i. 262.
[4] *Opuscula Mythologica* (Amst. 1688).

beliefs from nation to nation, to fetish-worship, to
the worship of the heavenly bodies, to the deification
of dead men.   In an essay like the present, dealing
only with a fragment of this great inquiry, it will
be safest to take the most general view, and to say
that man's fear and wonder invest every object, real
or imaginary, which strongly impresses him,—beasts
or stones, or souls and spirits, or fire and the sun in
heaven,—with an intelligence and a power darkly
resembling his own ; and, moreover, that certain
phenomena, real or supposed,—dreams and epilepsy,
eclipse and thunder, sorceries and the uprising of
the dead,—recur from time to time to supply him
with apparent proof of the validity of his beliefs,
and to modify those beliefs according to the nature
of his country and his daily life.   Equally natural
is it that, as his social instincts develop and his
power of generalisation begins, he will form such
conceptions as those of a moral government of the
world, of a retributory hereafter, of a single Power
from which all others emanate, or into which they
disappear.

Avoiding, therefore, any attempt to take a side
among conflicting theories, I will draw from the
considerations which follow no further moral than
one which is well-nigh a truism, though too often
forgotten in the heat of debate, namely, that we are
assuredly not as yet in a position to pass a final
judgment on the forms which religion has assumed

in the past; we have traversed too small a part of
the curve of human progress to determine its true
character; even yet, in fact, "we are ancients of the
earth, and in the morning of the times." The difficulty of bearing this clearly in mind, great in every
age, becomes greater as each age advances more
rapidly in knowledge and critical power. In this
respect the eighteenth century teaches us an obvious
lesson. That century witnessed a marked rise in
the standard of historical evidence, a marked enlightenment in dealing with the falsities and superstitions of the past. The consequence was that all
things seemed explicable; that whatever could not
be reduced to ordinary rules seemed only worthy of
being brushed aside. Since that day the standard
of evidence in history has not declined,—it has
become stricter still; but at the same time the
need of sympathy and insight, if we would comprehend the past, has become strongly felt, and has
modified or suspended countless judgments which
the philosophers of the last century delivered without misgiving. The difference between the two
great critics and philosophers of France, at that day
and in our own, shows at a glance the whole gulf
between the two points of view. How little could
the readers of Voltaire have anticipated Renan!
How little could they have imagined that their
master's trenchant arguments would so soon have
fallen to the level of half-educated classes and half-

civilised nations,—would have been formidable only in sixpenny editions, or when translated into Hindostani for the confutation of missionary zeal!

What philosophical enlightenment was in the last century, science, physical or historical, is in our own. Science is the power to which we make our first and undoubting appeal, and we run a corresponding risk of assuming that she can already solve problems wholly, which as yet she can solve only in part,—of adopting under her supposed guidance explanations which may hereafter be seen to have the crudity and one-sidedness of Voltaire's treatment of Biblical history.

The old school of theologians were apt to assume that because all men—or all men whom they chose to count—had held a certain belief, that belief must be true. Our danger lies rather in being too ready to take for granted that when we have explained how a belief arose we have done with it altogether; that because a tenet is of savage parentage it hardly needs formal disproof. In this view the wide diffusion of a belief serves only to stamp its connection with uncivilised thought, and "quod semper, quod ubique, quod ab omnibus," has become to many minds rather the badge of superstition than the test of catholic truth. That any one but ourselves should have held a creed seems to lower the average intelligence of its adherents.

Yet, on behalf of savages, and our ancestors in

general, there may be room for some apology. If
we reflect how large a part of human knowledge
consists of human emotion, we may even say that
they possessed some forms of knowledge which we
have since lost. The mind of man (it has been
well said), like the earth on which he walks, under-
goes perpetual processes of denudation as well as of
deposit. We ourselves, as children, did in a sense
know much which we know no more; our picture
of the universe, incomplete and erroneous as it was,
wore some true colours which we cannot now recall.
The child's vivid sensibility, reflected in his vivifying
imagination, is as veritably an inlet of truth as if
it were an added clearness of physical vision; and
though the child himself has not judgment enough
to use his sensibilities aright, yet if the man is to
discern the poetic truth about Nature, he will need
to recall to memory his impressions as a child.

Now, in this way too, the savage is a kind of
child; his beliefs are not always to be summarily
referred to his ignorance; there may be something
in them which we must realise in imagination before
we venture to explain it away. Ethnologists have
recognised the need of this difficult self-identification
with the remote past, and have sometimes remarked,
with a kind of envy, how much nearer the poet is
than the philosopher to the savage habit of mind.

There is, however, one ancient people in whose
case much of this difficulty disappears, whose re-

ligion may be traced backwards through many
phases into primitive forms, while yet it is easy to
study its records with a fellow-feeling which grows
with our knowledge till it may approach almost to
an identity of spirit.　Such is the ascendency which
the great works of the Greek imagination have established over the mind of man, that it is no paradox
to say that the student's danger lies often in excess
rather than in defect of sympathy.　He is tempted
to ignore the real superiority of our own religion,
morality, civilisation, and to re-shape in fancy an
adult world on an adolescent ideal.　But the remedy
for over-estimates, as well as for under-estimates,
lies in an increased definiteness of knowledge, an
ever-clearer perception of the exact place in the
chain of development which Greek thought and
worship hold.　The whole story of Greek mythology
must ere long be retold in a form as deeply modified
by comparative ethnology as our existing treatises
have been modified by comparative philology.　Such
a task would be beyond my powers ; but while
awaiting some more comprehensive treatment of the
subject by a better-qualified hand, I have in this
Essay endeavoured to trace,—by suggestion rather
than in detail, but with constant reference to the
results of recent science, — the development and
career in Greece of one remarkable class of religious
phenomena which admits to some extent of separate
treatment.

Greek oracles reflect for a thousand years [1] the spiritual needs of a great people. They draw their origin from an Animism [2] which almost all races share, and in their early and inarticulate forms they contain a record of most of the main currents in which primitive beliefs are wont to run. Afterwards—closely connected both with the idea of supernatural possession and with the name of the sun-god Apollo—they exhibit a singular fusion of nature-worship with Shahmanism or sorcery. Then, as the non-moral and naturalistic conception of the deity yields to the moral conception of him as an idealised man, the oracles reflect the change, and the Delphian god becomes in a certain sense the conscience of Greece.

A period of decline follows; due, as it would seem, partly to the depopulation and political ruin of Greece, but partly also to the indifference or scepticism of her dominant schools of philosophy. But this decline is followed by a revival which forms one of the most singular of those apparent checks which complicate the onward movement of thought by ever new modifications of the beliefs of the remote past. So far as this complex movement

[1] Roughly speaking, from 700 B.C. to 300 A.D., but the earliest oracles probably date much farther back.

[2] It is hardly necessary to say that by Animism is meant a belief in the existence around us of souls or spirits, whether disembodied, as ghosts, or embodied in fetishes, animals, etc. Shahmanism is a word derived from the title of the Siberian wizards, who procure by agitated trance some manifestation from their gods.

can be at present understood, it seems to have been
connected among the mass of the people with the
wide-spread religious upheaval of the first Christian
centuries, and to have been at last put an end to by
Christian baptism or sword.   Among the higher
minds it seems to have rested partly on a perplexed
admission of certain phenomena, partly on the
strongly-felt need of a permanent and elevated revelation, which yet should draw its origin from the
Hellenic rather than the Hebrew past.   And the
story reaches a typical conclusion in the ultimate
disengagement of the highest natures of declining
Greece from mythology and ceremonial, and the
absorption of definite dogma into an overwhelming
ecstasy.

II.

The attempt to define the word "oracle" con-
fronts us at once with the difficulties of the subject.
The Latin term, indeed, which we are forced to
employ, points specially to cases where the voice of
God or spirit was actually heard, whether directly
or through some human intermediary.   But the
corresponding Greek term (μαντεῖον) merely signifies
a seat of soothsaying, a place where divinations are
obtained by whatever means.   And we must not
regard the oracles of Greece as rare and majestic
phenomena, shrines founded by a full-grown mythology for the direct habitation of a god.   Rather they

are the products of a long process of evolution, the modified survivals from among countless holy places of a primitive race.

Greek literature has preserved to us abundant traces of the various causes which led to the ascription of sanctity to some particular locality. Oftenest it is some chasm or cleft in the ground, filled, perhaps, with mephitic vapours, or with the mist of a subterranean stream, or merely opening in its dark obscurity an inlet into the mysteries of the underworld. Such was the chasm of the Clarian,[1] the Delian,[2] the Delphian Apollo; and such the oracle of the prophesying nymphs on Cithæron.[3] Such was Trophonius' cave,[4] and his own name perhaps is only a synonym for the Mother Earth, "in many names the one identity," who nourishes at once and reveals.[5]

Sometimes—as for instance at Megara,[6] Sicyon, Orchomenus, Laodicea—the sanctity gathers around some βαίτυλος or fetish-stone, fashioned, it may be,

---

[1] Iambl. de Myst. p. 74.

[2] Lebègue, Recherches sur Délos, p. 89.

[3] Paus. ix. 3. See also Paus. v. 14, for a legend of an oracle of Earth herself at Olympia.

[4] Paus. ix. 39.

[5] Τροφώνιος from τρέφω. The visitor, who lay a long time, οὐ μάλα συμφρονῶν ἐναργῶς εἴτ' ἐγρήγορεν εἴτ' ὠνειροπόλει (Plut. de Genio Socratis, 22), had doubtless been partially asphyxiated. St. Patrick's Purgatory was perhaps conducted on the same plan.

[6] Paus. i. 43, and for further references on bætyls see Lebègue, p. 85. See also Lubbock, Origin of Civilisation, p. 225.

into a column or pyramid, and probably in most
cases identified at first with the god himself, though,
after the invention of statuary, its significance might
be obscured or forgotten.   Such stones outlast all
religions, and remain for us in their rude shapeless-
ness the oldest memorial of the aspirations or the
fears of man.

Sometimes the sacred place was merely some
favourite post of observation of the flight of birds,
or of lightning, like Teiresias' "ancient seat of
augury,"[1] or the hearth[2] from which, before the
sacred embassy might start for Delphi, the Pythaists
watched above the crest of Parnes for the summons
of the heavenly flame.

Or it might be merely some spot where the
divination from burnt-offerings seemed unusually
true and plain,—at Olympia, for instance, where, as
Pindar tells us, "soothsayers divining from sacrifice
make trial of Zeus who lightens clear."   It is needless to speak at length of groves and streams and
mountain-summits, which in every region of the
world have seemed to bring the unseen close to man
by waving mystery, or by rushing murmur, or by
nearness to the height of heaven.[3]   It is enough to

---

[1] Soph. *Ant.* 1001 ; Paus. ix. 16 ; and cf. Eur. *Phoen.* 841.

[2] Strabo, ix. p. 619. They watched ἀπὸ τῆς ἐσχάρας τοῦ ἀστραπαίου
Διός. See also Eur. *Ion.* 295. Even a place where lots were custom-
arily drawn might become a seat of oracle.—Paus. vii. 25.

[3] There is little trace in Greece of "weather-oracles,"— such as
the Blocksberg,—hills deriving a prophetic reputation from the

undeistand that in Greece, as in other countries over which successive waves of immigration have passed, the sacred places were for the most part selected for primitive reasons, and in primitive times; then as more civilised races succceded and Apollo came,— whence or in what guise cannot here be discussed, —the old shrines were dedicated to new divinities, the old symbols were metamorphosed or disappeared. The fetish-stones were crowned by statues, or replaced by statues and buried in the earth.[1] The Sibyls died in the temples, and the sun-god's island holds the sepulchre of the moon-maidens of the northern sky.[2]

It is impossible to arrange in quite logical order phenomena which touch each other at so many points, but in making our transition from these impersonal or hardly personal oracles of divination to the "voice-oracles"[3] of classical times, we may

indications of coming rain, etc., drawn from clouds on their summits. The sanctity of Olympus, as is well known, is connected with a supposed elevation above all elemental disturbances.

[1] Pind. *Ol.* viii. 3, and for further references see Hermann, *Griech. Ant.* ii. 247. Maury (ii. 447) seems to deny this localisation on insufficient grounds.

[2] The Hyperboreæ, see reff. ap. Lebègue, p. 69. M. Bouché-Leclercq's discussion (vol. ii.) of the Sibylline legends is more satisfactory than that of Klausen (*Aeneas und die Penaten*, p. 107, foll.) He describes the Sibylline type as "une personnification gracieuse de la mantique intuitive, intermédiaire entre le babil inconscient de la nymphe Écho et la sagacité inhumaine de la Sphinx."

[3] Χρησμοὶ φθεγματικοί.

first mention the well-known Voice or Rumour
which as early as Homer runs heaven-sent through
the multitude of men, or sometimes prompts to
revolution by "the word of Zeus."[1]

To this we may add the belief that words
spoken at some critical and culminant, or even at
some arbitrarily-chosen moment, have a divine significance. We find some trace of this in the oracle
of Teiresias,[2] and it appears in a strange form in
an old oracle said to have been given to Homer,
which tells him to beware of the moment when
some young children shall ask him a riddle which
he is unable to answer.[3] Cases of omens given by
a chance word in classical times are too familiar
to need further reference.[4] What we have to
notice here is, that this casual method of learning the will of heaven was systematised into a
practice at certain oracular temples, where the
applicant made his sacrifice, stopped his ears, went
into the market-place, and accepted the first words

---

[1] ὄσσα, φήμη, κληδών, ὀμφή—Il. ii. 93; Herod. ix. 100 ; Od. iii.
215, etc. These words are probably used sometimes for regular
oracular communications.

[2] Od. xi. 126.

[3] ἀλλὰ νέων παίδων αἴνιγμα φύλαξαι. Paus. x. 24; Anth. Pal.
xiv. 66. This conundrum, when it was at length put to Homer,
was of so vulgar a character that no real discredit is reflected on
the Father of Poetry by his perplexity as to its solution. (Homeri
et Hesiodi certamen, ad fin.) Heraclitus, however, used the fact
to illustrate the limitation of even the highest human powers.

[4] Herodotus ix. 91, may be selected as an example of a happy
chance in forcing an omen.

he happened to hear as a divine intimation. We hear of oracles on this pattern at Memphis,[1] and at Pharæ in Achæa.[2]

From these voices, which, though clearly audible, are, as it were, unowned and impersonal, we may pass to voices which have a distinct personality, but are heard only by the sleeping ear. Dreams of departed friends are likely to be the first phenomenon which inspires mankind with the idea that they can hold converse with a spiritual world. We find dreams at the very threshold of the theology of almost all nations, and accordingly it does not surprise us to find Homer asserting that dreams come from Zeus,[3] or painting, with a pathos which later literature has never surpassed, the strange vividness and agonising insufficiency of these fugitive visions of the night.[4]

And throughout Greek literature presaging dreams which form, as Plutarch says, "an unfixed and wandering oracle of Night and Moon"[5] are

---

[1] Dio Chrys. *ad Alex.* 32, 13, παῖδες ἀπαγγέλλουσι παίζοντες τὸ δοκοῦν τῷ θεῷ.

[2] Paus. vii. 22.

[3] *Il.* i. 63. Or from Hermes, or earth, or the gods below.

[4] *Il.* xxiii. 97. If we accept the theory of an older Achilleid we find the importance of augury proper decreasing, of dreams increasing, in the Homeric poems themselves. Geddes, *Hom. Probl.* p. 186 ; cf. Mure, *Hist. Gr. Lit.* i. 492. Similarly Apollo's darts grow more gentle, and his visitations more benign. — Geddes, p. 140.

[5] Plut. *Ser. Num. Vind.* 22.

abundant in every form, from the high behest laid
on Bellerophon "when in the dark of night stood
by him the shadowy-shielded maid, and from a
dream, suddenly, a waking vision she became,"[1]
down to the dreams in the temples of Serapis or of
Aesculapius which Aristides the Rhetorician has
embalmed for us in his Sacred Orations,—the
dream which "seemed to indicate a bath, yet not
without a certain ambiguity," or the dream which
left him in distressing uncertainty whether he were
to take an emetic or no.[2]

And just as we have seen that the custom of
observing birds, or of noting the omens of casual
speech, tended to fix itself permanently in certain
shrines, so also dream-oracles, or temples where the
inquirer slept in the hope of obtaining an answer
from the god seen in vision, or from some other
vision sent by him, were one of the oldest forms of
oracular seats. Brizo, a dream-prophetess, preceded
Apollo at Delos.[3] A similar legend contrasts "the
divination of darkness" at Delphi with Apollo's clear
prophetic song.[4] Night herself was believed to send
visions at Megara,[5] and coins of Commodus still
show us her erect and shrouded figure, the torches
that glimmer in her shade. Amphiaraus,[6] Amphilo-

---

[1] Pind. Ol. xiii. 100.

[2] Ar. Rhet. vol. i. p. 275 (Dind.), ἔχον μέν τινα ἔννοιαν λουτροῦ,
οὐ μέντοι χωρὶς γε ὑπονοίας, and i. 285.

[3] Athen. viii. 2, and see Lebègue, p. 218; comp. Aesch. Ag. 275.

[4] Eur. Iph. Taur. 1234 foll. [5] Paus. i. 40. [6] Paus. i. 34.

chus,[1] Charon,[2] Pasiphae,[3] Herakles,[4] Dionysus,[5] and above all Asklepios,[6] gave answers after this fashion, mainly, but not entirely, in cases of sickness. The prevalence of heroes, rather than gods, as the givers of oracles in dreams seems still further to indicate the immediate derivation of this form of revelation from the accustomed appearance of departed friends in sleep.

The next step takes us to the most celebrated class of oracles,—those in which the prophetess, or more rarely the prophet, gives vent in agitated trance to the words which she is inspired to utter.[7] We encounter here the phenomena of possession, so familiar to us in the Bible, and of which theology still maintains the genuineness, while science would explain them by delirium, hysteria, or epilepsy. It

---

[1] Dio Cass. lxxii. 7.

[2] Eustath. *Schol. ad Dionys. Perieg.* 1153.

[3] Cic. *de Div.* i. 43 ; Plut. *Agis* 9, and cf. Maury, ii. 453.

[4] Paus. ix. 24, comp. inscr. ap. G. Wolff, *de Noviss.* p. 29, and see Plut. *de Malign. Herod.* 31, for the dream of Leonidas in Herakles' temple.   [5] Paus. x. 33.

[6] Ar. Rhet. *passim;* Iambl. *Myst.* 3, 3, etc.   See also Val. Max. i. 7 ; Diod. Sic. v. 62 ; Ar. Rhet. *Sacr. Serm.* iii. 311, for dreams sent by Athene, the Soteres, Hemithea.   Further references will be found in Maury, iii. 456, and for the relation of Apollo to dreams see Bouché-Leclercq, i. 204.

[7] Pindar's phrase (for the prophecy of Iamus), φωνὰν ἀκούειν ψευδέων ἄγνωστον, *Ol.* vi. 66, reminds us of Socrates' inward monitor. The expressions used about the Pythia vary from this conception of mere *clairaudience* to the idea of an absolute *possession,* which for the time holds the individuality of the prophetess entirely in abeyance.

was this phenomenon, connected first, as Pausanias tells us,[1] with the Apolline oracles, which gave a wholly new impressiveness to oracular replies. No longer confined to simple affirmation and negation, or to the subjective and ill-remembered utterances of a dream, they were now capable of embracing all topics, and of being preserved in writing as a revelation of general applicability. These oracles of inspiration, — taken in connection with the oracles uttered by visible phantoms, which become prominent at a later era,—may be considered as marking the highest point of development to which Greek oracles attained. It will be convenient to defer our consideration of some of these phenomena till we come to the great controversy between Porphyry and Eusebius, in which they were for the first time fully discussed. But there is one early oracle of the dead, different in some respects from any that succeeded it,[2] which presents so many points for notice that a

[1] Paus. i. 34. We should have expected this prophetic frenzy to have been connected with Bacchus or the Nymphs rather than with Apollo, and it is possible that there may have been some transference of the phenomena from the one worship to the other. The causes which have determined the attributes of the Greek deities are often too fanciful to admit of explanation now.

[2] The distinction drawn by Nägelsbach between this and other "Todtenorakeln" (*Nachhom. Theologie*, p. 189) is surely exaggerated. See Klausen, *Aeneas und die Penaten*, p. 129 foll., for other legends connecting Odysseus with early necromancy, and on this general subject see Herod. v. 92 ; Eur. *Alc.* 1131 ; Plat. *Leg.* x. 909 ; Plut. *Cim.* 6, *de Ser. Num. Vind.* 17 ; Tylor, *Prim. Cult.* ii. 41. The fact, on which Nägelsbach dwells, that Odysseus, after

few reflections on the state of belief which it indicates will assist us in comprehending the nature of
the elevation of Greek faith which was afterwards
effected under the influence of Delphi.

For this,—the first oracle of which we have a
full account, — the descent of Odysseus to the
underworld, "to consult the soul of the Theban
Teiresias," shows in a way which it would be hard
to parallel elsewhere the possible co-existence in the
same mind of the creed and practices of the lowest
races with a majesty, a pathos, a power, which
human genius has never yet overpassed.   The
eleventh book of the Odyssey is steeped in the
Animism of barbarous peoples.   The Cimmerian
entrance to the world of souls is the close parallel
(to take one instance among many) of the extreme
western cape of Vanua Levi, a calm and solemn
place of cliff and forest, where the souls of the
Fijian dead embark for the judgment - seat of
Ndengei, and whither the living come on pilgrim-
age, thinking to see ghosts and gods.[1]   Homer's
ghosts cheep and twitter precisely as the shadow-

consulting Teiresias, satisfied his affection and his curiosity by
interviews with other ghosts in no way alters the original injunction laid on him, the purport of his journey—ψυχῇ χρησόμενον
Θηβαίου Τειρεσίαο. Nägelsbach's other argument, that in later times
we hear only of a dream-oracle, not an apparition-oracle, of Teiresias seems to me equally weak. Readers of Pausanias must surely
feel what a chance it is which has determined the oracles of which
we *have* heard.

[1] *Prim. Cult.* i. 408.

souls of the Algonquin Indians chirp like crickets, and Polynesian spirits speak in squeaking tones, and the accent of the ancestral Zulu, when he reappears on earth, has earned for him the name of Whistler.[1] The expedition of Odysseus is itself paralleled by the exploit of Ojibwa, the eponymous hero of the Ojibbeways, of the Finnish hero Wainamoinen, and of many another savage chief. The revival of the ghosts with blood, itself closely paralleled in old Teutonic mythologies,[2] speaks of the time when the soul is conceived as feeding on the fumes and shadows of earthly food, as when the Chinese beat the drum which summons ancestral souls to supper, and provide a pail of gruel and a spoon for the greater convenience of any ancestor who may unfortunately have been deprived of his head.[3]

Nay, even the inhabitants of that underworld are only the semblances of once living men. " They themselves," in the terrible words of the opening sentence of the Iliad, " have been left a prey to dogs and every bird." Human thought has not yet reached a point at which spirit could be conceived of as more than the shadow of matter.

And if further evidence were needed, the oracle of Teiresias himself—opening like a chasm into Hades through the sunlit soil of Greece—reveals unwittingly all the sadness which underlies that freshness and power, the misgiving which so often

---

[1] *Prim. Cult.* ii. 42.　　　[2] *Ibid.* ii. 346.　　　[3] *Ibid.* ii. 30.

unites the savage and the philosopher, the man who comes before religions and the man who comes after them, in the gloom of the same despair. Himself alone in his wisdom among the ineffectual shades, Teiresias offers to Odysseus, in the face of all his unjust afflictions, no prevention and no cure; "of honey-sweet return thou askest, but by God's will bitter shall it be;"—for life's struggle he has no remedy but to struggle to the end, and for the wandering hero he has no deeper promise than the serenity of a gentle death.

And yet Homer "made the theogony of the Greeks."[1] And Homer, through the great ages which followed him, not only retained, but deepened his hold on the Hellenic spirit. It was no mere tradition, it was the ascendency of that essential truth and greatness in Homer, which we still so strongly feel, which was the reason why he was clung to and invoked and explained and allegorised by the loftiest minds of Greece in each successive age; why he was transformed by Polygnotus, transformed by Plato, transformed by Porphyry. Nay, even in our own day,—and this is not the least significant fact in religious history,—we have seen one of the most dominant, one of the most religious intellects of our century, falling under the same spell, and extracting from Homer's almost savage

---

[1] Herod. ii. 53, οὗτοι δέ (Homer and Hesiod) εἰσι οἱ ποιήσαντες θεογονίην Ἕλλησι, κ.τ. λ.

animism the full-grown mysteries of the Christian faith.

So dangerous would it be to assume such a congruence throughout the whole mass of the thought of any epoch, however barbarous, that the baseness or falsity of some of its tenets should be enough to condemn the rest unheard. So ancient, so innate in man is the power of apprehending by emotion and imagination aspects of reality for which a deliberate culture might often look in vain. To the dictum,—so true though apparently so para- doxical,—which asserts "that the mental condition of the lower races is the key to poetry," we may reply with another apparent paradox—that poetry is the only thing which every age is certain to recog- nise as truth.

Having thus briefly considered the nature of each of the main classes of oracular response, it is natural to go on to some inquiry into the history of the leading shrines where these responses were given. The scope of this essay does not admit of a detailed notice of each of the very numerous oracular seats of which some record has reached us.[1] But before passing on to Delphi, I must dwell on two cases of special interest, where recent explorations have brought us nearer than elsewhere to what may be

[1] The number of Greek oracular seats, with the Barbarian seats known to the Greeks, has been estimated at 260, or an even larger number; but of very many of these we know no more than the name.

called the private business of an oracle, or to the actual structure of an Apolline sanctuary.

The oracle of Zeus at Dodona takes the highest place among all the oracles which answered by signs rather than by inspired speech.[1]   It claimed to be the eldest of all, and we need not therefore wonder that its phenomena present an unusual confluence of streams of primitive belief.   The first mention of Dodona,[2]—in that great invocation of Achilles which is one of the glimpses which Homer gives us of a world far earlier than his own,—seems to indicate that it was then a seat of dream-oracles, where the rude Selloi perhaps drew from the earth on which they slept such visions as she sends among men. But in the Odyssey[3] and in Hesiod[4] the oracle is spoken of as having its seat among the leaves, or in the hollow or base of an oak, and this is the idea which prevailed in classical times.[5]   The doves,[6]— if doves there were, and not merely priestesses, whose name, Peleiades, may be derived from some other root,[7]—introduce another element of complexity.

---

[1] Strab. viii. *Fragm.* ἐχρησμῴδει δ' οὐ διὰ λόγων ἀλλὰ διά τινων συμβόλων, ὥσπερ τὸ ἐν Λιβύῃ Ἀμμωνιακόν.   So Suid. *in voc.* Δωδώνη, etc.   [2] *Il.* xvi. 233.

[3] *Od.* xiv. 327, xix. 296.

[4] Hes. *Fr.* 39. 7, ναῖόν τ' ἐν πυθμένι φηγοῦ.   See Plat. *Phaedr.* 275.

[5] Aesch. *Prom.* 832 ; Soph. *Trach.* 172 and 1167.

[6] See Herod. ii. 54, and comp. *Od.* xii. 63.

[7] See Herm. *Griech. Antiq.* ii. 250.   Dr. Robertson Smith suggests "that the Dove-soothsayers were so named from their *croon* . . . and that the μέλισσα (the Pythia) in like manner is the humming priestess." —*Journal of Philology,* vol. xiv. p. 120.

Oracles were also given at Dodona by means of
lots,[1] and by the falling of water.[2] Moreover, German industry has established the fact, that at
Dodona it thunders on more days than anywhere
else in Europe, and that no peals are louder anywhere
than those which echo among the Acroceraunian
mountains. It is tempting to derive the word
Dodona from the sound of a thunderclap, and to
associate this old Pelasgic sanctuary with the pro-
pitiation of elemental deities in their angered hour.[3]
But the notices of the oracle in later days are per-
plexingly at variance with all these views. They
speak mainly of oracles given by the sound of caldrons, — struck, according to Strabo,[4] by knuckle-

---

[1] Cic. *de Div.* ii. 32.   [2] Serv. *ad Aen.* iii. 466.

[3] I do not think that we can get beyond some such vague conjecture as this, and A. Mommsen and Schmidt's elaborate calculations as to months of maximum frequency of thunderclaps and
centres of maximum frequency of earthquakes, as determining the
time of festivals or the situation of oracular temples, seem to me
to be quite out of place. If a savage possessed the methodical
patience of a German observer, he would be a savage no more.
Savants must be content to leave Aristotle's τύχη καὶ τὸ αὐτόματον,
—chance and spontaneity,—as causes of a large part of the action
of primitive men.

The dictum of Götte (*Delphische Orakel*, p. 13) seems to me
equally unprovcable : " Dodona, wohin die schwarzen aegyptischen
Tauben geflogen kamen, ist wohl unbestreitbar eine aegyptische
Cultstätte, die Schwesteranstalt von Ammonium, beide Thebens
Töchter." The geographical position of Dodona is much against
this view, the doves are very problematical, and the possible ex-
istence of a primitive priesthood in the Selloi is no proof of an
Egyptian influence.

[4] Strab. lib. vii. *Fragm.* ap. Hermann, *Griech. Ant.* ii. 251,
where see further citations.

bones attached to a wand held by a statue. The
temple is even said to have been *made* of caldrons,[1]
or at least they were so arranged, as a certain Demon
tells us,[2] that "all in turn, when one was smitten,
the caldrons of Dodona rang." The perpetual sound
thus caused is alluded to in a triumphant tone by
other writers,[3] but it is the more difficult to determine
in what precise way the will of Zeus was understood.

Among such a mass of traditions, it is of course
easy to find analogies. The doves may be compared
to the hissing ducks of the Abipones, which were
connected with the souls of the dead,[4] or with the

---

[1] Steph. Byz. *s. voc.* Δωδώνη, quoted by Carapanos, in whose
monograph on Dodona citations on all these points will be found.

[2] Müller, *Fragm. Hist. Gr.* iii. 125.

[3] Callim. *Hymn. in Del.* 286 ; Philostr. *Imag.* ii. 33 (a slightly
different account).

[4] *Prim. Cult.* ii. 6. The traces of animal worship in Greece are
many and interesting, but are not closely enough connected with
our present subject to be discussed at length. Apollo's possible
characters, as the Wolf, the Locust, or the Fieldmouse (or the
Slayer of wolves, of locusts, or of fieldmice), have not perceptibly
affected his oracles. Still less need we be detained by the fish-tailed
Eurynome, or the horse-faced Demeter (Paus. viii. 41, 42). And
although from the time when the boy-prophet Iamus lay among
the wall-flowers, and "the two bright-eyed serpents fed him with
the harmless poison of the bee" (Pind. *Ol.* vi. 28), snakes appear
frequently in connection with prophetic power, their worship falls
under the head of divination rather than of oracles. The same
remark may be made of ants, cats, and cows. The bull Apis occu-
pies a more definite position, but though he was visited by Greeks,
his worship was not a product of Greek thought. The nearest
Greek approach, perhaps, to an animal-oracle was at the fount of
Myræ in Cilicia (Plin. *H.N.* xxxii. 2), where fish swam up to eat
or reject the food thrown to them. "Diripere eos carnes objectas

doves in Popayan, which are spared as inspired by
departed souls.   The tree-worship opens up lines of
thought too well known for repetition.   We may
liken the Dodonæan "voiceful oak" to the tamarisks
of Beersheba, and the oak of Shechem,—its whisper
to the "sound of a going in the tops of the mul-
berry-trees," which prompted Israel to war,[1] and so
on down the long train of memories to Joan of Arc
hanging with garlands the fairies' beech in the woods
of Domremy, and telling her persecutors that if they
would set her in a forest once more she would hear
the heavenly voices plain.[2]   Or we may prefer,
with another school, to trace this tree also back to
the legendary Ygdrassil, "the celestial tree of the
Aryan family," with its spreading branches of the
stratified clouds of heaven.   One legend at least
points to the former interpretation as the more
natural.   For just as a part of the ship Argo, keel
or prow, was made of the Dodonæan oak, and Argo's
crew heard with astonishment the ship herself prophesy to them on the sea :—

lactum est consultantibus," says Pliny, "caudis abigere dirum."
The complaint of a friend of Plutarch's (*Quæst. conviv.* iv. 4) "that
it was impossible to obtain from fishes a single instructive look or
sound," is thus seen to have been exaggerated.   And it appears
that live snakes were kept in the cave of Trophonius (Philostr. *Vit.
Apoll.* viii. 19), in order to inspire terror in visitors, who were
instructed to appease them with cakes (Suid. *s. v.* μελιτοῦττα).

[1] 2 Sam. v. 24.

[2] "Dixit quod si esset in uno nemore bene audiret voces venientes
ad eam."—On Tree-worship, see Lubbock, *Origin of Civilisation,*
p. 206 foll.

"But Jason and the builder, Argus, knew
　　Whereby the prow foretold things strange and new ;
Nor wondered aught, but thanked the gods therefore,
　　As far astern they left the Mysian shore," [1]—

so do we find a close parallel to this among the
Siamese,[2] who believe that the inhabiting nymphs
of trees pass into the guardian spirits of boats built
with their wood, to which they continue to sacrifice.

Passing on to the answers which were given at
this shrine, we find that at Dodona,[3] as well as at
Delphi,[4] human sacrifice is to be discerned in the
background. But in the form in which the legend
reaches us, its horror has been sublimed into pathos.
Coresus, priest of Bacchus at Calydon, loved the
maiden Callirhoe in vain. Bacchus, indignant at
his servant's repulse, sent madness and death on
Calydon. The oracle of Dodona announced that
Coresus must sacrifice Callirhoe, or some one who
would die for her. No one was willing to die for
her, and she stood up beside the altar to be slain.
But when Coresus looked on her his love overcame
his anger, and he slew himself in her stead. Then
her heart turned to him, and beside the fountain to
which her name was given she died by her own
hand, and followed him to the underworld.

---

[1] Morris' *Life and Death of Jason*, Book iv. *ad fin.*
[2] *Prim. Cult.* ii. 198.　　　　　　[3] Paus. vii. 21.
[4] Eus. *Pr. Ev.* v. 27, παρθένον Αἰπυτίδαν κλῆρος καλεῖ, etc. See
also the romantic story of Melanippus and Comætho, Paus. vii. 19.

There is another legend of Dodona[1] to which the student of oracles·may turn with a certain grim satisfaction at the thought that the ambiguity of style which has so often baffled him did once at least carry its own penalty with it. Certain Bœotian envoys, so the story runs, were told by Myrtile, the priestess of Dodona, "that it would be best for them to do the most impious thing possible." The Bœotians immediately threw the priestess into a caldron of boiling water, remarking that they could not think of anything much more impious than *that*.

The ordinary business of Dodona, however, was of a less exciting character. M. Carapanos has discovered many tablets on which the inquiries of visitors to the oracle were inscribed, and these give a picture, sometimes grotesque, but oftener pathetic, of the simple faith of the rude Epirots who dwelt round about the shrine. The statuette of an acrobat hanging to a rope shows that the "Dodonæan Pelasgian Zeus" did not disdain to lend his protection to the least dignified forms of jeopardy to life and limb. A certain Agis asks "whether he has lost his blankets and pillows himself, or some one outside has stolen them." An unknown woman asks simply how she may be healed of her disease. Lysanias asks if he is indeed the father of the child which his wife Nyla is soon to bear. Evandrus and his

---

[1] Ephor. ad Strab. ix. 2 ; Heracl. Pont. *Fragm. Hist. Gr.* ii. 198 ; Proclus, *Chrest.* ii. 248, and see Carapanos.

wife, in broken dialect, seek to know "by what prayer or worship they may fare best now and for ever." And there is something strangely pathetic in finding on a broken plate of lead the imploring inquiry of the fierce and factious Corcyreans,—made, alas! in vain,—"to what god or hero offering prayer and sacrifice they might live together in unity?"[1] "For the men of that time," says Plato,[2] "since they were not wise as ye are nowadays, it was enough in their simplicity to listen to oak or rock, if only these told them true." To those rude tribes, indeed, their voiceful trees were the one influence which lifted them above barbarism and into contact with the surrounding world. Again and again Dodona was ravaged,[3] but so long as the oak was standing the temple rose anew. When at last an Illyrian bandit cut down the oak[4] the presence of Zeus was gone, and the desolate Thesprotian valley has known since then no other sanctity, and has found no other voice.

I proceed to another oracular seat, of great mythical celebrity, though seldom alluded to in classical times, to which a recent exploration[5] has given a striking interest, bringing us, as it were, into direct connection across so many ages with the birth and advent of a god.

---

[1] Τίνι κα θεῶν ἢ ἡρώων θύοντες καὶ ὠχόμενοι ὁμονοοῖεν ἐπὶ τἀγαθόν.

[2] Phaedr. 275.

[3] Strab. vii. 6 ; Polyb. ix. 67, and cf. Wolff, *de Noviss.* p. 13.

[4] Serv. *ad Aen.* iii. 466.

[5] *Recherches sur Délos*, par J. A. Lebègue, 1876.

On the slope of Cynthus, near the mid-point of
the Isle of Delos, ten gigantic blocks of granite,
covered with loose stones and the débris of ages,
form a rude vault, half hidden in the hill. The
islanders call it the "dragon's cave;" travellers had
taken it for the remains of a fortress or of a reser-
voir. It was reserved for two French savants to
show how much knowledge the most familiar texts
have yet to yield when they are meditated on by
minds prepared to compare and to comprehend. A
familiar passage in Homer,[1] illustrated by much
ancient learning and by many calculations of his
own, suggested to M. Burnouf, Director of the French
School of Archæology at Athens, that near this point
had been a primitive post of observation of the
heavens; nay, that prehistoric men had perhaps
measured their seasons by the aid of some rude
instrument in this very cave. An equally familiar
line of Virgil,[2] supported by some expressions in a
Homeric hymn, led M. Lebègue to the converging
conjecture that at this spot the Delian oracle had
its seat; that here it was that Leto's long wanderings ended, and Apollo and Artemis were born.
Every schoolboy has learnt by heart the sounding
lines which tell how Aeneas "venerated the temple
built of ancient stone," and how at the god's unseen
coming "threshold and laurel trembled, and all the

[1] *Od.* xv. 403. Em. Burnouf, *Revue Archéologique*, Aug. 8, 1873.
[2] *Aen.* iii. 84; Hom. *Hymn. Del.* 15-18, and 79-81.

mountain round about was moved." But M. Lebègue
was the first to argue hence with confidence that the
oracle must have been upon the mountain and not
on the coast, and that those ancient stones, like the
Cyclopean treasure-house of Mycenæ, might be found
and venerated still. So far as a reader can judge
without personal survey, these expectations have
been amply fulfilled.[1] At each step M. Lebègue's
researches revealed some characteristic of an oracular
shrine. In a walled external space were the remains of a marble base on which a three-legged
instrument had been fixed by metal claws. Then
came a transverse wall, shutting off the temple
within, which looks westward, so that the worshipper,
as he approaches, may face the east. The floor of
this temple is reft by a chasm,—the continuation of
a ravine which runs down the hill, and across which
the sanctuary has been intentionally built. And in
the inner recess is a rough block of granite, smoothed
on the top, where a statue has stood. The statue
has probably been knocked into the chasm by a rock
falling through the partly-open roof. Its few fragments show that it represented a young god. The
stone itself is probably a fetish, surviving, with the
Cyclopean stones which make the vault above it,

[1] M. Homolle (*Fouilles de Délos*, 1879) gives no direct opinion
on the matter, but his researches indirectly confirm M. Lebègue's
view, in so far as that among the numerous inscriptions, etc., which
he has found among the ruins of the temple of Apollo on the coast,
there seems to be no trace of oracular response or inquiry.

from a date perhaps many centuries before the
Apolline religion came. This is all, but this is
enough. For we have here in narrow compass all
the elements of an oracular shrine; the westward
aspect, the sacred enclosure, the tripod, the sanctuary, the chasm, the fetish-stone, the statue of a
youthful god. And when the situation is taken into
account, the correspondence with the words both of
Virgil and of the Homerid becomes so close as to be
practically convincing. It is true that the smallness
of scale,—the sanctuary measures some twenty feet
by ten,—and the remote archaism of the structure,
from which all that was beautiful, almost all that
was Hellenic, has long since disappeared, cause at
first a shock of disappointment like that inspired by
the size of the citadel, and the character of the
remains at Hissarlik. Yet, on reflection, this seem-
ing incongruity is an additional element of proof.
There is something impressive in the thought that
amidst all the marble splendour which made Delos
like a jewel in the sea, it was this cavernous and
prehistoric sanctuary, as mysterious to Greek eyes
as to our own, which their imagination identified
with that earliest temple which Leto promised, in
her hour of trial, that Apollo's hands should build.
This, the one remaining seat of oracle out of the
hundreds which Greece contained, was the one sanctuary which the Far-darter himself had wrought;—
no wonder that his mighty workmanship has out-

lasted the designs of men! All else is gone. The temples, the amphitheatres, the colonnades, which glittered on every crest and coign of the holy island, have sunk into decay. But he who sails among the isles of Greece may still watch around sea-girt Delos " the dark wave welling shoreward beneath the shrill and breezy air;"[1] he may still note at sunrise, as on that sunrise when the god was born, " the whole island abloom with shafts of gold, as a hill's crested summit blooms with woodland flowers."[2] "And thou thyself, lord of the silver bow," he may exclaim with the Homerid in that burst of exultation in which the uniting Ionian race seems to leap to the consciousness of all its glory in an hour,—" thou walkedst here in very presence, on Cynthus' leafy crown !"

"Ah, many a forest, many a peak is thine,
On many a promontory stands thy shrine,
But best and first thy love, thy home, is here ;
Of all thine isles thy Delian isle most dear ;—
There the long-robed Ionians, man and maid,
Press to thy feast in all their pomp arrayed,—
To thee, to Artemis, to Leto pay
The heartfelt honour on thy natal day ;—
Immortal would he deem them, ever young,
Who then should walk the Ionian folk among,
Should those tall men, those stately wives behold,
Swift ships seafaring and long-garnered gold :—

---

[1] *Hymn. Del.* 27.   [2] *Ibid.* 138-164.

> But chiefliest far his eyes and ears would meet
> Of sights, of sounds most marvellously sweet,
> The Delian girls amid the thronging stir,
> The loved hand-maidens of the Far-darter ;
> The Delian girls, whose chorus, long and long,
> Chants to the god his strange, his ancient song,—
> Till whoso hears it deems his own voice sent
> Thro' the azure air that music softly blent,
> So close it comes to each man's heart, and so
> His own soul feels it and his glad tears flow."

Such was the legend of the indigenous, the Hellenic
Apollo.   But the sun does not rise over one horizon
alone, and the glory of Delos was not left uncon-
tested or unshared.   Another hymn, of inferior
poetical beauty, but of equal, if not greater, authority
among the Greeks, relates how Apollo descended
from the Thessalian Olympus, and sought a place
where he might found his temple: how he was
refused by Tilphussa, and selected Delphi ; and how,
in the guise of a dolphin, he led thither a crew of
Cretans to be the servants of his shrine.   With this
hymn, so full of meaning for the comparative mytho-
logist, we are here only concerned as introducing us
to Apollo in the aspect in which we know him best,
" giving his answers from the laurel-wood, beneath
the hollows of Parnassus' hill."[1]

At Delphi, as at Dodona, we seem to trace the
relics of many a form of worship and divination
which we cannot now distinctly recall.   From that

[1] *Hymn. Pyth.* 214.

deep cleft "in rocky Pytho," Earth, the first prophetess, gave her earliest oracle,[1] in days which were
already a forgotten antiquity to the heroic age of
Greece. The maddening vapour, which was supposed
to rise from the chasm,[2] belongs to nymph-inspira-
tion rather than to the inspiration of Apollo. At
Delphi, too, was the most famous of all fetish-
stones, believed in later times to be the centre of
the earth.[3]   At Delphi divination from the sacrifice
of goats reached an immemorial antiquity.[4]   Delphi,
too, was an ancient centre of divination by fire, a
tradition which survived in the name of Pyrcon,[5]
given to Hephaestus' minister, while Hephaestus
shared with Earth the possession of the shrine, and
in the mystic title of the Flame-kindlers,[6] assigned
in oracular utterances to the Delphian folk. At
Delphi, too, in ancient days, the self-moved lots

---

[1] Aesch. *Eum.* 2 ; Paus. x. 5 ; cf. Eur. *Iph. Taur.* 1225 *sqq.*

[2] Strabo, ix. p. 419, etc. In a paper read before the British
Archæological Association, March 5, 1879, Dr. Phenè has given an
interesting account of subterranean chambers at Delphi, which
seem to indicate that gases from the subterranean Castalia were
received in a chamber where the Pythia may have sat. But in the
absence of direct experiment this whole question is physiologically
very obscure. It is even possible, as M. Bouché-Leclercq urges,
that the Pythia's frenzy may be a survival from a previous
Dionysiac worship at Delphi, and thus originally traceable to a
quite orthodox intoxicant.

[3] Paus. x. 16, etc.

[4] Diod. Sic. xvi. 26. Pliny (*Hist. Nat.* vii. 56) ascribes the invention of this mode of divination to Delphos, a son of Apollo.

[5] Paus. x. 5.

[6] Plut. *Pyth.* 24.

sprang in the goblet in obedience to Apollo's will.[1]
The waving of the Delphic laurel,[2] which in later
times seemed no more than a token of the wind and
spiritual stirring which announced the advent of
the god, was probably the relic of an ancient tree-
worship, like that of Dodona,[3] and Daphne, priestess
of Delphi's primeval Earth-oracle,[4] is but one more
of the old symbolical figures that have melted back
again into impersonal nature at the appearing of
the God of Day. Lastly, at Delphi is laid the
scene of the sharpest conflict between the old gods
and the new. Whatever may have been the meaning of the Python,—whether he were a survival of
snake-worship, or a winding stream which the sun's
rays dry into rotting marsh, or only an emblem of
the cloud which trails across the sunlit heaven,—
his slaughter by Apollo was an integral part of the
early legend, and at the Delphian festivals the
changes of the " Pythian strain " commemorated for
many a year that perilous encounter,—the god's
descent into the battlefield, his shout of summons,

---

[1] Suidas, iii. p. 237; cf. Callim. *Hymn. in Apoll.* 45, etc.

[2] Ar. *Plut.* 213 ; Callim. *Hymn. in Apoll.* 1, etc.

[3] I cannot, however, follow M. Maury (*Religions de la Grèce*, ii.
442) in supposing (as he does in the case of the Delian laurel, *Aen.*
iii. 73) that such tree-movements need indicate an ancient habit of
divining from their sound. The idea of a wind accompanying
divine manifestations seems more widely diffused in Greece than
the Dodonæan idea of vocal trees. Cf. (for instance) Plut. *De Def.
orac.* of the Delphian adytum, εὐωδίας ἀναπίμπλαται καὶ πνεύματος.

[4] Paus. x. 5.

his cry of conflict, his paean of victory, and then
the gnashing of the dragon's teeth in his fury, the
hiss of his despair.[1]   And the mythology of a later
age has connected with this struggle the first ideas
of moral conflict and expiation which the new
religion had to teach; has told us that the victor
needed purification after his victory; that he endured and was forgiven; and that the god himself
first wore his laurel-wreath as a token of supplica-
tion, and not of song.[2]

With a similar ethical purpose the simple narrative of the Homerid has been transformed into a
legend[3] of a type which meets us often in the
middle ages, but which wears a deeper pathos when
it occurs in the midst of Hellenic gladness and
youth,—the legend of Trophonius and Agamedes,
the artificers who built the god's home after his
heart's desire, and whom he rewarded with the
guerdon that is above all other recompense, a speedy
and a gentle death.

In the new temple at any rate, as rebuilt in
historic times, the moral significance of the Apolline
religion was expressed in unmistakable imagery.
Even as " four great zones of sculpture " girded the
hall of Camelot, the centre of the faith which was

---

[1] ἄμπειρα, κατακελευσμός, σάλπιγξ, δάκτυλοι, ὀδοντισμός, σύριγγες.
See August Mommsen's *Delphika* on this topic.

[2] Bötticher, *Baumcultus*, p. 353 ; and see reff. ap. Herm. *Griech.
Ant.* ii. 127.   Cf. Eur. *Ion,* 114 *sqq.*

[3] Cic. *Tusc.* i. 47; cf. Plut. *De Consol. ad Apollon.* 14.

civilising Britain, "with many a mystic symbol" of the victory of man, so over the portico of the Delphian god were painted or sculptured such scenes as told of the triumph of an ideal humanity over the monstrous deities which are the offspring of savage fear.[1]

There was "the light from the eyes of the twin faces" of Leto's children; there was Herakles with golden sickle, Iolaus with burning brand, withering the heads of the dying Hydra,—"the story," says the girl in the *Ion* who looks thereon, "which is sung beside my loom;" there was the rider of the winged steed slaying the fire-breathing Chimaera; there was the tumult of the giants' war; Pallas lifting the aegis against Enceladus; Zeus crushing Mimas with the great bolt fringed with flame, and Bacchus "with his unwarlike ivy-wand laying another of Earth's children low."

It is important thus to dwell on some of the indications,—and there are many of them,—which point to the conviction entertained in Greece as to the ethical and civilising influence of Delphi, inasmuch as the responses which have actually been preserved to us, though sufficient, when attentively considered, to support this view, are hardly such as would at once have suggested it. The set collections

---

[1] The passage in the *Ion*, 190-218, no doubt describes either the portico which the Athenians dedicated at Delphi about 426 B.C. (Paus. x. 11), or (as the words of the play, if taken strictly, would indicate) the façade of the temple itself.

of oracles, which no doubt contained those of most
ethical importance, have perished ; of all the "dark-
written tablets, groaning with many an utterance of
Loxias,"[1] none remain to us except such fragments
of Porphyry's treatise as Eusebius has embodied in
his refutation.   And many of the oracles which we
do possess owe their preservation to the most trivial
causes,—to their connection with some striking anecdote, or to something quaint in their phraseology
which has helped to make them proverbial.   The
reader, therefore, who passes from the majestic
descriptions of the *Ion* or the *Eumenides* to the
actual study of the existing oracles will at first run
much risk of disappointment.   Both style and subject will often seem unworthy of these lofty claims.
He will come, for instance, on such oracles as that
which orders Temenus to seek as guide of the army
a man with three eyes, who turns out (according to
different legends) to be either a one-eyed man on a
two-eyed horse, or a two-eyed man on a one-eyed
mule.[2]   This oracle is composed precisely on the
model of the primitive riddles of the Aztec and the
Zulu, and is almost repeated in Scandinavian legend,
where Odin's single eye gives point to the enigma.[3]
Again, the student's ear will often be offended by

---

[1] Eur. *Fr.* 625.   Collections of oracles continued to be referred
to till the Turks took Constantinople, *i.e.* for about 2000 years.
See reff. ap. Wolff, *de Noviss.* p. 48.

[2] Apollod. ii. 8 ; Paus. v. 3.   [3] *Prim. Cult.* i. 85.

roughnesses of rhythm which seem unworthy of the
divine inventor of the hexameter.[1]   And the con-
stantly-recurring prophecies are, for the most part,
uninteresting and valueless, as the date of their
composition cannot be proved, nor their genuineness
in any way tested.   As an illustration of the kind
of difficulties which we here encounter, we may
select one remarkable oracle,[2] of immense celebrity
in antiquity, which certainly suggests more questions
than we can readily answer.   The outline of the
familiar story is as follows:—Crœsus wished to
make war on Cyrus, but was afraid to do so without
express sanction from heaven.   It was therefore
all-important to him to test the veracity of the
oracles, and his character, as the most religious man
of his time, enabled him to do so systematically,
without risk of incurring the charge of impiety.
He sent messages to the six best-known oracles then
existing,—to Delphi, to Dodona, to Branchidae, to
the oracles of Zeus Ammon, of Trophonius, of
Amphiaraus.   On the hundredth day from leaving
Sardis, his envoys were to ask what Crœsus was at
that moment doing.   Four oracles failed; Amphi-

[1] Bald though the god's style may often be, he possesses at any
rate a sounder notion of metre than some of his German critics.
Lobeck (*Aglaophamus*, p. 852), attempting to restore a lost response,
suggests the line

στενυγρὴν δ'ἐνοεῦν εὐρυγάστορα οὐ κατὰ γαῖαν.

He apologises for the quantity of the first syllable of εὐρυγάστορα,
but seems to think that no further remark is needed.

[2] Herod. i. 47.

araus was nearly right; Apollo at Delphi entirely
succeeded.   For the Pythia answered, with exact
truth, that Crœsus was engaged in boiling a lamb
and a tortoise together in a copper vessel with a
copper lid.   The messengers, who had not themselves known what Crœsus was going to do, returned
to Sardis and reported, and were then once more
despatched to Delphi, with gifts so splendid that
in the days of Herodotus they were still the glory
of the sanctuary.   They now asked the practically
important question as to going to war, and received
a quibbling answer which, in effect, lured on Crœsus
to his destruction.

Now here the two things certain are that
Crœsus did send these gifts to Delphi, and did go
to war with Cyrus.   Beyond these facts there is no
sure footing.   Short and pithy fragments of poetry,
like the oracles on which the story hangs, are
generally among the earliest and most enduring
fragments of genuine history.   On the other hand,
they are just the utterances which later story-tellers
are most eager to invent.   Nor must we argue from
their characteristic diction, for the pseudo-oracular
is a style which has in all ages been cultivated
with success.   The fact which it is hardest to dis-
pose of is the existence of the prodigious, the
unrivalled offerings of Crœsus at Delphi.   Why
were they sent there, unless for some such reason
as Herodotus gives?   Or are they sufficiently ex-

plained by a mere reference to that almost superstitious deference with which the Mermnadae seem
to have regarded the whole religion and civilisation
of Greece ? With our imperfect data, we can perhaps hardly go with safety beyond the remark that,
granting the genuineness of the oracle about the
tortoise, and the substantial truth of Herodotus'
account, there will still be no reason to suppose
that the god had any foreknowledge as to the result
of Crœsus' war. The story itself, in fact, contains
almost a proof to the contrary. We cannot suppose
that the god, in saying, " Crœsus, if he cross the
Halys, shall undo a mighty realm," was intentionally inciting his favoured servant to his ruin. It is
obvious that he was sheltering his ignorance behind
a calculated ambiguity. And the only intelligence
to which he or his priestess could, on any hypothesis,
fairly lay claim, would be of the kind commonly
described as " second-sight," a problem with which
ethnologists have already to deal all over the world,
from the Hebrides to the Coppermine River.

It is obvious that the documents before us are
far from enabling us to prove even this hypothesis.
And we are farther still from any evidence for
actual prophecy which can stand a critical investi-
gation. Hundreds of such cases are indeed reported
to us, and it was on a conviction that Apollo did
indeed foretell the future that the authority of
Delphi mainly depended. But when we have said

this, we have said all; no case is so reported as to
enable us altogether to exclude the possibility of
coincidence, or of the fabrication of the prophecy
after the event.   But, on the other hand,—and this
is a more surprising circumstance,—it is equally
difficult to get together any satisfactory evidence for
the conjecture which the parallel between Delphi
and the Papacy so readily suggests, — that the
power of the oracle was due to the machinations of
a priestly aristocracy, with widely-scattered agents,
who insinuated themselves into the confidence, and
traded on the credulity, of mankind.   We cannot
but suppose that, to some extent at least, this must
have been the case ; that when "the Pythia philip-
pised" she reflected the fears of a knot of Delphian
proprietors ; that the unerring counsel given to
private persons, on which Plutarch insists, must
have rested, in part at least, on a secret acquaint-
ance with their affairs, possibly acquired in some
cases under the seal of confession.   In the paucity,
however, of direct evidence to this effect, our
estimate of the amount of pressure exercised by a
deliberate human agency in determining the policy
of Delphi must rest mainly on our antecedent view
of what is likely to have been the case, where the
interests involved were of such wide importance.[1]

---

[1] For this view of the subject, see Hüllmann, *Würdigung des
Delphischen Orakels ;* Götte, *Das Delphische Orakel.* August
Mommsen (*Delphika*) takes a somewhat similar view, and calls the
Pythia a "blosse Figurantin," but his erudition has added little

For indeed the political influence of the Delphian oracle, however inspired or guided,—the value to Hellas of this one unquestioned centre of national counsel and national unity, — has always formed one of the most impressive topics with which the historian of Greece has had to deal.   And I shall pass this part of my subject rapidly by, as already familiar to most readers, and shall not repeat at length the well-known stories,—the god's persistent command to expel the Peisistratids from Athens, his partiality for Sparta, as shown both in encouragement and warning,[1] or the attempts, successful[2] and unsuccessful,[3] to bribe his priestess.   Nor shall I do more than allude to the encouragement of colonisation, counsel of great wisdom, which the god lost no opportunity of enforcing on both the Dorian and the Ionian stocks.   He sent the Cretans to Sicily,[4] and Alcmaeon to the Echinades;[5] he ordered the foundation of Byzantium[6] " over against the city of the blind;" he sent Archias to Ortygia to

to the scanty store of texts on which Hüllmann, etc., depend.   I may mention here that Hendess has collected most of the existing oracles (except those quoted by Eusebius) in a tract, *Oracula quae supersunt*, etc., which is convenient for reference.

[1] Herod. vi. 52; Thuc. i. 118, 123; ii. 54.   Warnings, ap. Paus. iii. 8; ix. 32; Diod. Sic. xi. 50; xv. 54.   Plut. *Lys.* 22; *Agesil.* 3.

[2] Cleisthenes, Herod. v. 63, 66; Pleistoanax, Thuc. v. 16.

[3] Lysander; Plut. *Lys.* 26; Ephor. *Fr.* 127; Nep. *Lys.* 3.   See also Herod. vi. 66.

[4] Herod. vii. 170.   [5] Thuc. ii. 102.

[6] Strab. vii. 320; Tac. *Ann.* xii. 63; but see Herod. iv. 144.

found Syracuse,[1] the Bœotians to Heraclea at Pratos,[2] and the Spartans to Heraclea in Thessaly. And in the story which Herodotus[3] and Pindar[4] alike have made renowned, he singled out Battus,— anxious merely to learn a cure for his stammer, but type of the man with a destiny higher than he knows,—to found at Cyrene "a charioteering city upon the silvern bosom of the hill." And, as has often been remarked, this function of colonisation had a religious as well as a political import. The colonists, before whose adventurous armaments Apollo, graven on many a gem, still hovers over the sea, carried with them the civilising maxims of the "just-judging"[5] sanctuary as well as the brand kindled on the world's central altar-stone from that pine-fed[6] and eternal fire. Yet more distinctly can we trace the response of the god to each successive stage of ethical progress to which the evolution of Greek thought attains.

The moralising Hesiod is honoured at Delphi in preference to Homer himself. The Seven Wise Men, the next examples of a deliberate effort after ethical rules, are connected closely with the Pythian shrine. Above the portal is inscribed that first condition of all moral progress, "Know Thyself";

---

[1] Paus. v. 7.   [2] Justin. xvi. 3.
[3] Herod. iv. 155.   [4] *Pyth.* iv.
[5] *Pyth.* xi. 9.
[6] Plut. *de EI apud Delphos.* Cf. Aesch. *Eum.* 40 ; *Choeph.* 1036.

nor does the god refuse to encourage the sages
whose inferior ethical elevation suggests to them
only such maxims as, "Most men are bad," or
"Never go bail."[1]

Solon and Lycurgus, the spiritual ancestors of
the Athenian and the Spartan types of virtue, receive the emphatic approval of Delphi, and the
"Theban eagle," the first great exponent of the developed faith of Greece, already siding with the
spirit against the letter, and refusing to ascribe to
a divinity any immoral act, already preaching the
rewards and punishments of a future state in strains
of impassioned revelation,—this great poet is dear
above all men to Apollo during his life, and is
honoured for centuries after his death by the priest's
nightly summons, "Let Pindar the poet come in to
the supper of the god."[2] . It is from Delphi that
reverence for oaths, respect for the life of slaves, of
women, of suppliants, derive in great measure their
sanction and strength.[3]   I need only allude to the
well-known story of Glaucus, who consulted the
god to know whether he should deny having received the gold in deposit from his friend, and who
was warned in lines which sounded from end to end
of Greece of the nameless Avenger of the broken

---

[1] I say nothing *de EI apud Delphos*, about the mystic word
which five of the wise men, or perhaps all seven together, put up
in wooden letters at Delphi, for their wisdom has in this instance
wholly transcended our interpretation.

[2] Paus. ix. 23.   [3] Herod. ii. 134 ; vi. 139, etc.

oath,—whose wish was punished like a deed, and whose family was blotted out. The numerous responses of which this is the type brought home to men's minds the notion of right and wrong, of reward and punishment, with a force and impressiveness which was still new to the Grecian world.

More surprising, perhaps, at so early a stage of moral thought, is the catholicity of the Delphian god, his indulgence towards ceremonial differences or ceremonial offences, his reference of casuistical problems to the test of the inward rightness of the heart.[1] It was the Pythian Apollo who replied to the inquiry, "How best are we to worship the gods?" by the philosophic answer, "After the custom of your country,"[2] and who, if those customs varied, would only bid men choose "the best." It was Apollo who rebuked the pompous sacrifice of the rich Magnesian by declaring his preference for the cake and frankincense which the pious Achæan offered in humbleness of heart.[3] It was Apollo who

---

[1] See, for instance, the story of the young man and the brigands, Ael. *Hist. Var.* iii. 4. 3.

[2] Xen. *Mem.* iv. 3. ἥ τε γὰρ Πυθία νόμῳ πόλεως ἀναιρεῖ ποιοῦντας εὐσεβῶς ἂν ποιεῖν. The Pythia often urged the maintenance or renewal of ancestral rites. Paus. viii. 24, etc.

[3] Theopomp. *Fr.* 283 ; cf. Sopater, *Prolegg. in Aristid. Panath.* p. 740, εὐαδέ μοι χθιζὸς λίβανος, κ.τ.λ. (Wolff, *de Noviss.* p. 5; Lob, *Agl.* 1006), and compare the story of Poseidon (Plut. *de Prof. in Virt.* 12), who first reproached Stilpon in a dream for the cheapness of his offerings, but on learning that he could afford nothing

warned the Greeks not to make superstition an excuse for cruelty ; who testified, by his commanding interference, his compassion for human infirmities, for the irresistible heaviness of sleep,[1] for the thoughtlessness of childhood,[2] for the bewilderment of the whirling brain.[3]

Yet the impression which the Delphian oracles make on the modern reader will depend less on isolated anecdotes like these than on something of the style and temper which appears especially in those responses which Herodotus has preserved,— something of that delightful mingling of *naïveté* with greatness, which was the world's irrecoverable bloom. What scholar has not smiled over the god's answer[4] to the colonists who had gone to a barren island in mistake for Libya, and came back complaining that Libya was unfit to live in ? He told them that " if they who had never visited the

better, smiled, and promised to send abundant anchovies. For the Delphian god's respect for honest poverty, see Plin. *H. N.* vii. 47.

[1] Evenius. Herod. ix. 93.

[2] Paus. viii. 23. This is the case of the Arcadian children who hung the goddess in play.

[3] Paus. vi. 9 ; Plut. *Romul.* 28 (Cleomedes). For further instances of the inculcation of mercy, see Thuc. ii. 102 ; Athen. xi. p. 504.

[4] Herod. iv. 157. There seems some analogy between this story and the Norse legend of second-sight, which narrates how "Mgimund shut up three Finns in a hut for three nights that they might visit Iceland and inform him of the lie of the country where he was to settle. Their bodies became rigid, they sent their souls on the errand, and awakening after three days, they gave a description of the Vatnsdael."— *Prim. Cult.* i. 396.

sheep-bearing Libya knew it better than he who
had, he greatly admired their cleverness." Who
has not felt the majesty of the lines which usher
in the test-oracle of Croesus with the lofty assertion of the omniscience of heaven?[1] lines which
deeply impressed the Greek mind, and whose graven
record, two thousand years afterwards, was among
the last relics which were found among the ruins of
Delphi.[2]

It is Herodotus, if any one, who has caught for
us the expression on the living face of Hellas.   It
is Herodotus whose pencil has perpetuated that
flying moment of young unconsciousness when evil
itself seemed as if it could leave no stain on her
expanding soul, when all her faults were reparable,
and all her wounds benign ; when we can still feel
that in her upward progress all these and more
might be forgiven and pass harmless away—

> " For the time
> Was May-time, and as yet no sin was dreamed."

And through all this vivid and golden scene the
Pythian Apollo—" the god," as he is termed with a
sort of familiar affection—is the never-failing coun-
sellor and friend.   His providence is all the divinity
which the growing nation needs.   His wisdom is

---

[1] Herod. i. 47.

[2] Cyriac of Ancona, in the sixteenth century, found a slab of
marble with the couplet οἶδα τ' ἐγώ, etc., inscribed on it.   See
Fourart, p. 139.

not inscrutable and absolute, but it is near and
kind; it is like the counsel of a young father to
his eager boy. To strip the oracles from Herodotus' history would be to deprive it of its deepest
unity and its most characteristic charm.

And in that culminating struggle with the barbarians, when the young nation rose, as it were, to
knightly manhood through one great ordeal, how
moving — through all its perplexities — was the
attitude of the god! We may wish, indeed, that
he had taken a firmer tone, that he had not trembled
before the oncoming host, nor needed men's utmost
supplications before he would give a word of hope.
But this is a later view; it is the view of Oenomaus
and Eusebius, rather than of Aeschylus or Herodotus.[1] To the contemporary Greeks it seemed no
shame nor wonder that the national protector,
benignant but not omnipotent, should tremble with
the fortunes of the nation, that all his strength
should scarcely suffice for a conflict in which every
fibre of the forces of Hellas was strained, "as
though men fought upon the earth and gods in
upper air."

And seldom indeed has history shown a scene
so strangely dramatic, never has poetry entered so
deeply into human fates, as in that council at
Athens[2] when the question of absolute surrender

---

[1] Herod. vii. 139, seems hardly meant to blame the god, though
it praises the Athenians for hoping against hope.

[2] Herod. vii. 143.

or desperate resistance turned on the interpretation which was to be given to the dark utterance of the god. It was an epithet which saved civilisation; it was the one word which blessed the famous islet instead of cursing it altogether, which gave courage for that most fateful battle which the world has known—

> "Thou, holy Salamis, sons of men shalt slay,
> Or on earth's scattering or ingathering day."

After the great crisis of the Persian war Apollo is at rest.[1] In the tragedians we find him risen high above the attitude of a struggling tribal god. Worshippers surround him, as in the *Ion*, in the spirit of glad self-dedication and holy service; his priestess speaks as in the opening of the *Eumenides*, where the settled majesty of godhead breathes through the awful calm. And now, more magnificent though more transitory than the poet's song, a famous symbolical picture embodies for the remaining generations of Greeks the culminant conception of the religion of Apollo's shrine.

"Not all the treasures," as Homer has it, "which the stone threshold of the Far-darter holds safe within" would now be so precious to us as the power of looking for one hour on the greatest work of the greatest painter of antiquity, the picture by

---

[1] It is noticeable that the god three times defended his own shrine,—against Xerxes (Herod. viii. 36), Jason of Pherae (Xen. *Hell.* vi. 4), Brennus (Paus. x. 23).

Polygnotus in the Hall of the Cnidians at Delphi,
of the descent of Odysseus among the dead.[1]　For
as it was with the oracle of Teiresias that the roll
of responses began, so it is the picture of that same
scene which shows us, even through the meagre
description of Pausanias, how great a space had
been traversed between the horizon and the zenith
of the Hellenic faith.　"The ethical painter," as
Aristotle calls him,[2] the man on whose works it
ennobled a city to gaze, the painter whose figures
were superior to nature as the characters of Homer
were greater than the greatness of men, had spent
on this altar-piece, if I may so term it, of the
Hellenic race his truest devotion and his utmost
skill.　The world to which he introduces us is
Homer's shadow-world, but it reminds us also of a
very different scene.　It recalls the visions of that
Sacred Field on whose walls an unknown painter
has set down with so startling a reality the faith of
mediæval Christendom as to death and the hereafter.

In place of Death with her vampire aspect and
wiry wings, we have the fiend Eurynomus, "painted
of the blue-black colour of flesh-flies," and battening

---

[1] For this picture see Paus. x. 28-31 ; also Welcker (*Kleine
Schriften*), and W. W. Lloyd in the Classical Museum, who both
give Riepenhausen's restoration.　While differing from much in
Welcker's view of the picture, I have followed him in supposing
that a vase figured in his *Alte Denkmäler*, vol. iii. plate 29, represents at any rate the figure and expression of Polygnotus' *Odysseus*.
The rest of my description can, I think, be justified from Pausanias.

[2] Ar. *Pol.* viii. 8 ; *Poet.* ii. 2.

on the corpses of the slain. In place of the kings
and ladies, who tell us in the rude Pisan epigraph
how

> " Ischermo di savere e di richezza
> Di nobiltate ancora e di prodezza
> Vale niente ai colpi de costei,"—

it is Theseus and Sisyphus and Eriphyle who teach
us that might and wealth and wisdom " against
those blows are of no avail." And Tityus, whose
scarce imaginable outrage in the Pythian valley
upon the mother of Apollo herself carries back his
crime and his penalty into an immeasurable past,—
Tityus lay huge and prone upon the pictured field,
but the image of him (and whether this were by
chance or art Pausanius could not say) seemed melt-
ing into cloud and nothingness through the infinity
of his woe. But there also were heroes and heroines
of a loftier fate,—Memnon and Sarpedon, Tyro and
Penthesilea, in attitudes that told that "calm pleasures
there abide, majestic pains ;"—Achilles, with Patro-
clus at his right hand, and near Achilles Protesilaus,
fit mate in valour and in constancy for that type of
generous friendship and passionate woe. And there
was Odysseus, still a breathing man, but with no
trace of terror in his earnest and solemn gaze, de-
manding from Teiresias, as Dante from Virgil, all
that that strange world could show ; while near him
a woman's figure stood, his mother Anticleia, waiting to call to him in those words which in Homer's

song seem to strike at once to the very innermost of all love and all regret. And where the mediæval painter had set hermits praying as the type of souls made safe through their piety and their knowledge of the divine, the Greek had told the same parable after another fashion. For in Polygnotus' picture it was Tellis and Cleoboia, a young man and a maid, who were crossing Acheron together with hearts at peace ; and amid all those legendary heroes these figures alone were real and true, and of a youth and a maiden who not long since had passed away ; and they were at peace because they had themselves been initiated, and Cleoboia had taught the mysteries of Demeter to her people and her father's house. And was there, we may ask, in that great company, any heathen form which we may liken, however distantly, to the Figure who, throned among the clouds on the glowing Pisan wall, marshals the blessed to their home in light? Almost in the centre, as it would seem, of Polygnotus' picture was introduced a mysterious personality who found no place in Homer's poem,—a name round which had grown a web of hopes and emotions which no hand can disentangle now, — " The minstrel sire of song, Orpheus the well-beloved, was there."

It may be that the myth of Orpheus was at first nothing more than another version of the world-old story of the Sun; that his descent and resurrection were but the symbols of the night and the day;

that Eurydice was but an emblem of the lovely rose-clouds which sink back from his touch into the darkness of evening only to enfold him more brightly in the dawn. But be this as it may, the name of Orpheus [1] had become the centre of the most aspiring and the deepest thoughts of Greece; the lyre which he held, the willow-tree on which in the picture his hand was laid, were symbols of mystic meaning, and he himself was the type of the man " who has descended and ascended "— who walks the earth with a heart that turns continually towards his treasure in a world unseen.

When this great picture was painted, the sanctuary and the religion of Delphi might well seem indestructible and eternal. But the name of Orpheus, introduced here perhaps for the first time into the centre of the Apolline faith, brings with it a hint of that spirit of mysticism which has acted as a solvent,—sometimes more powerful even than criticism, as the sun in the fable of Aesop was more powerful than the wind,—upon the dogmas of every religion in turn. And it suggests a forward glance to an oracle given at Delphi on a later day,[2] and cited by Porphyry to illustrate the necessary evanescence and imperfection of whatsoever image

---

[1] See, for instance, Maury, *Religions de la Grèce*, chap. xviii. Aelius Lampridius (*Alex. Sev. Vita*, 29) says—"In Larario et Apollonium et Christum, Abraham et Orpheum, et hujusmodi deos habebat."

[2] Eus. *Pr. Ev.* vi. 3.

of spiritual things can be made visible on earth. A
time shall come when even Delphi's mission shall
have been fulfilled; and the god himself has predicted without despair the destruction of his holiest
shrine—

> " Ay, if ye bear it, if ye endure to know
> That Delphi's self with all things gone must go,
> Hear with strong heart the unfaltering song divine
> Peal from the laurelled porch and shadowy shrine.
> High in Jove's home the battling winds are torn,
> From battling winds the bolts of Jove are born ;
> These as he will on trees and towers he flings,
> And quells the heart of lions or of kings ;
> A thousand crags those flying flames confound,
> A thousand navies in the deep are drowned,
> And ocean's roaring billows, cloven apart,
> Bear the bright death to Amphitrite's heart.
> And thus, even thus, on some long-destined day,
> Shall Delphi's beauty shrivel and burn away,—
> Shall Delphi's fame and fane from earth expire
> At that bright bidding of celestial fire."

The ruin has been accomplished. All is gone, save
such cyclopean walls as date from days before
Apollo, such ineffaceable memories as Nature herself
has kept of the vanished shrine.[1] Only the Cory-
cian cave still shows, with its gleaming stalagmites,
as though the nymphs to whom it was hallowed
were sleeping there yet in stone ; the Phaedriades

---

[1] See Mr. Aubrey de Vere's *Picturesque Sketches in Greece and
Turkey* for a striking description of Delphian scenery. Other
details will be found in Foucart, pp. 113, 114 ; and cf. Paus. x. 33.

or Shining Crags still flash the sunlight from their
streams that scatter into air; and dwellers at
Castri still swear that they have heard the rushing
Thyiades keep their rout upon Parnassus' brow.

III.

Even while Polygnotus was painting the Lesche
of the Cnidians at Delphi a man was talking in the
Athenian market-place, from whose powerful individuality, the most impressive which Greece had
ever known, were destined to flow streams of influence which should transform every department
of belief and thought. In tracing the history of
oracles we shall feel the influence of Socrates mainly
in two directions; in his assertion of a personal and
spiritual relation between man and the unseen
world, an oracle not without us but within; and in
his origination of the idea of science, of a habit of
mind which should refuse to accept any explanation
of phenomena which failed to confer the power of
predicting those phenomena or producing them anew.
We shall find that, instead of the old acceptance of
the responses as heaven-sent mysteries, and the old
demands for prophetic knowledge or for guidance in
the affairs of life, men are more and more concerned
with the questions: How can oracles be practically
produced? and what relation between God and man
do they imply? But first of all, the oracle which

concerned Socrates himself, which declared him to
be the wisest of mankind, is certainly one of the
most noticeable ever uttered at Delphi. The fact
that the man on whom the god had bestowed this
extreme laudation, a laudation paralleled only by
the mythical words addressed to Lycurgus, should a
few years afterwards have been put to death for
impiety, is surely one of a deeper significance than
has been often observed. It forms an overt and
impressive instance of that divergence between the
law and the prophets, between the letter and the
spirit, which is sure to occur in the history of all religions, and on the manner of whose settlement the
destiny of each religion in turn depends. In this
case the conditions of the conflict are striking and
unusual.[1] Socrates is accused of failing to honour
the gods of the State, and of introducing new gods
under the name of demons, or spirits, as we must
translate the word, since the title of demon has
acquired in the mouths of the Fathers a bad signi-
fication. He replies that he *does* honour the gods
of the State, as he understands them, and that the
spirit who speaks with him is an agency which he
cannot disavow.

The first count of the indictment brings into
prominence an obvious defect in the Greek religion,

---

[1] On the trial of Socrates and kindred points see, besides Plato
(*Apol.*, *Phaed.*, *Euthyphr.*) and Xenophon (*Mem.*, *Apol.*), Diog.
Laert. ii. 40, Diod. Sic. xiv. 37, Plut. *De genio Socratis.*

the absence of any inspired text to which the orthodox could refer. Homer and Hesiod, men like ourselves, were the acknowledged authors of the theology of Greece ; and when Homer and Hesiod were respectfully received, but interpreted with rationalising freedom, it was hard to know by what canons to judge the interpreter. The second count opens questions which go deeper still. It was indeed true, though how far Anytus and Meletus perceived it we cannot now know, that the demon of Socrates indicated a recurrence to a wholly different conception of the unseen world, a conception before which Zeus and Apollo, heaven-god and sun-god, were one day to disappear. But who, except Apollo himself, was to pronounce on such a question ? It was he who was for the Hellenic race the source of continuous revelation; his utterances were a sanction or a condemnation from which there was no appeal. And in this debate his verdict for the defendant had been already given. We have heard of Christian theologians who are " more orthodox than the Evangelists." In this case the Athenian jurymen showed themselves more jealous for the gods' honour than were the gods themselves.

To us, indeed, Socrates stands as the example of the truest religious conservatism, of the temper of mind which is able to cast its own original convictions in an ancestral mould, and to find the last outcome of speculation in the humility of a trustful

faith.   No man, as is well known, ever professed a
more childlike confidence in the Delphian god than
he, and many a reader through many a century has
been moved to a smile which was not far from tears
at his account of his own mixture of conscientious
belief and blank bewilderment when the infallible
deity pronounced that Socrates was the wisest of
mankind.

A spirit balanced like that of Socrates could
hardly recur; and the impulse given to philosophical
inquiry was certain to lead to many questionings as
to the true authority of the Delphic precepts.   But
before we enter upon such controversies, let us trace
through some further phases the influence of the
oracles on public and private life.

For it does not appear that Delphi ceased to give
utterances on the public affairs of Greece so long as
Greece had public affairs worthy the notice of a god.
Oracles occur, with a less natural look than when
we met them in Herodotus, inserted as a kind of
unearthly evidence in the speeches of Aeschines and
Demosthenes.[1]   Hyperides confidently recommends
his audience to check the account which a messenger
had brought of an oracle of Amphiaraus by despatch-
ing another messenger with the same question to
Delphi.[2]   Oracles, as we are informed, foretold the

---

[1] *e.g.* Dem. *Meid.* 53 :—τῷ δήμῳ τῶν Ἀθηναίων ὁ τοῦ Διὸς σημαίνει,
etc.

[2] Hyper. *Euxen.* p. 8.

battle of Leuctra,[1] the battle of Chaeionea,[2] the destruction of Thebes by Alexander.[3] Alexander himself consulted Zeus Ammon not only on his own parentage but as to the sources of the Nile, and an ingenuous author regrets that, instead of seeking information on this purely geographical problem, which divided with Homer's birthplace the curiosity of antiquity, Alexander did not employ his prestige and his opportunities to get the question of the origin of evil set at rest for ever.[4] We hear of oracles given to Epaminondas,[5] to the orator Callistratus,[6] and to Philip of Macedon.[7] To Cicero the god gave advice which that sensitive statesman would have done well to follow,—to take his own character and not the opinion of the multitude as his guide in life.[8]

Nero, too, consulted the Delphian oracle, which pleased him by telling him to " beware of seventy-three,"[9] for he supposed that he was to reign till he reached that year. The god, however, alluded to the age of his successor Galba. Afterwards Nero,—grown to an overweening presumption which could brook no rival worship, and become, as we may say, Antapollo as well as Antichrist,—murdered certain men and cast them into the cleft of Delphi, thus

---

[1] Paus. ix. 14.   [2] Plut. *Dem.* 19.   [3] Diod. xvii. 10.
[4] Max. Tyr. *Diss.* 25.   [5] Paus. viii. 11.   [6] Lycurg. *Leocr.* 160.
[7] Diod. xvi. 91.
[8] Plut. *Cic.* 5.   [9] Suet. *Nero,* 38.

extinguishing for a time the oracular power.[1] Plutarch, who was a contemporary of Nero's, describes in several essays this lowest point of oracular fortunes. Not Delphi alone, but the great majority of Greek oracles, were at that time hushed, a silence which Plutarch ascribes partly to the tranquillity and depopulation of Greece, partly to a casual deficiency of Demons,—the immanent spirits who give inspiration to the shrines, but who are themselves liable to change of circumstances, or even to death.[2]

Whatever may have been the cause of this oracular eclipse, it was of no long duration. The oracle of Delphi seems to have been restored in the reign of Trajan; and in Hadrian's days a characteristic story shows that it had again become a centre of distant inquirers. The main preoccupation of that imperial scholar was the determination of Homer's birthplace, and he put the question in person to the Pythian priestess. The question had naturally been asked before, and an old reply, purporting to have been given to Homer himself, had already been engraved on Homer's statue in the sacred precinct.

---

[1] Dio Cass. lxiii. 14. Suetonius and Dio Cassius do not know why Nero destroyed Delphi; but some such view as that given in the text seems the only conceivable one.

[2] Plut. de Defect. orac. 11. We may compare the way in which Heliogabalus put an end to the oracle of the celestial goddess of the Carthaginians, by insisting on marrying her statue, on the ground that she was the Moon and he was the Sun.—Herodian, v. 6.

But on the inquiry of the sumptuous emperor the priestess changed her tone, described Homer as " an immortal siren," and very handsomely made him out to be the grandson both of Nestor and of Odysseus.[1] It was Hadrian, too, who dropped a laurel-leaf at Antioch into Daphne's stream, and when he drew it out there was writ thereon a promise of his imperial power. He choked up the fountain, that no man might draw from its prophecy such a hope again.[2] But Hadrian's strangest achievement was to found an oracle himself. The worshippers of Antinous at Antinoe were taught to expect answers from the deified boy : "They imagine," says the scornful Origen, " that there breathes from Antinous a breath divine."[3]

For some time after Hadrian we hear little of Delphi. But, on the other hand, stories of oracles of varied character come to us from all parts of the Roman world. The bull Apis, "trampling the un-showered grass with lowings loud," refused food from the hand of Germanicus, and thus predicted his approaching death.[4] Germanicus, too, drew the same dark presage from the oracle at Colophon of the Clarian Apollo.[5] And few oracular answers have

---

[1] Anth. Pal. xiv. 102 :—ἄγνωστον μ' ἐρέεις γενεῆς καὶ πατρίδος αἴης ἀμβροσίου Σειρῆνος, etc.

[2] Sozomen, *Hist. Eccl.* v. 19.

[3] Orig. *ad. Cels.* ap. Wolff, *de Noviss.* p. 43, where see other citations.

[4] Plin. viii. 46. [5] Tac. *Ann.* ii. 54.

been more impressively recounted than that which
was given to Vespasian by the god Carmel, upon
Carmel, while the Roman's dreams of empire were
still hidden in his heart. "Whatsoever it be, Vespasian, that thou preparest now, whether to build
a house or to enlarge thy fields, or to get thee servants for thy need, there is given unto thee a mighty ˙
home, and far-reaching borders, and a multitude of
men."[1]

The same strange mingling of classic and Hebrew
memories, which the name of Carmel in this connection suggests, meets us when we find the god Bel at
Apamea,—that same Baal "by whom the prophets
prophesied and walked after things that do not
profit" in Jeremiah's day, — answering a Roman
emperor in words drawn from Homer's song. For
it was thus that the struggling Macrinus received
the signal of his last and irretrievable defeat:[2]—

"Ah, king outworn ! young warriors press thee sore,
　And age is on thee, and thou thyself no more."

In the private oracles, too, of these post-classical
times there is sometimes a touch of romance which
reminds us how much human emotion there has

---

[1] Tac. *Hist.* ii. 78. Suetonius, *Vesp.* 5, speaks of Carmel's *oracle*,
though it seems that the answer was given after a simple *extispi-
cium*.

[2] Dio Cass. lxxviii. 40 ; Hom. *Il.* viii. 103. Capitolinus, in his
life of Macrinus (c. 3), shows incidentally that under the Antonines
it was customary for the Roman proconsul of Africa to consult the
oracle of the Dea Caelestis Carthaginiensium.

been in generations which we pass rapidly by; how earnest and great a thing many a man's mission has seemed to him, which to us is merged in the dulness and littleness of a declining age.   There is something of this pathos in the Pythia's message to the wandering preacher,[1] "Do as thou now doest, until thou reach the end of the world," and in the dream which came to the weary statesman in Apollo Grannus' shrine,[2] and bade him write at the end of his life's long labour Homer's words—

> "But Hector Zeus took forth and bare him far
> From dust, and dying, and the storm of war."

And in the records of these last centuries of paganism we notice that the established oracles, the orthodox forms of inquiry, are no longer enough to satisfy the eagerness of men.   In that upheaval of the human spirit which bore to the surface so much of falsehood and so much of truth,—the religion of Mithra, the religion of Serapis, the religion of Christ,—questions are asked from whatever source, glimpses are sought through whatsoever in nature has been deemed transparent to the influences of an encompassing Power.   It was in this age [3] that at

---

[1] Dio Chrysostom, περὶ φυγῆς, p. 255. This message had, perhaps, a political meaning.

[2] Dio Cassius, ad fin.; Hom. Il. xi. 163.

[3] The following examples of later oracles are not precisely synchronous. They illustrate the character of a long period, and the date at which we happen to hear of each has depended largely on accident.

Hierapolis the "clear round stone of the onyx kind," which Damascius describes, showed in its mirroring depths letters which changed and came, or sometimes emitted that "thin and thrilling sound,"[1] which was interpreted into the message of a slowly-uttering Power. It was in this age that Chosroes drew his divinations from the flickering of an eternal fire.[2] It was in this age that the luminous meteor would fall from the temple of Uranian Venus upon Lebanon into her sacred lake beneath, and declare her presence and promise her consenting grace.[3] It was in this age that sealed letters containing numbered questions were sent to the temple of the sun at Hierapolis, and answers were returned in order, while the seals remained still intact.[4] It was in this age that the famous oracle which predicted the death of Valens was obtained by certain men who sat round a table and noted letters of the alphabet

[1] Damasc. ap. Phot. 348, φωνὴν λεπτοῦ σιρίσματος. See also Paus. vii. 21, and compare Spartian, *Did. Jul.* 7, where a child sees the images in a mirror applied to the top of his head rendered abnormally sensitive by an unexplained process.

[2] Procop. *Bell. Pers.* ii. 24. The practice of divining from sacrificial flame or smoke was of course an old one, though rarely connected with any regular seat of oracle. Cf. Herod. viii. 134. The πυρεῖον in the χωρίον 'Αδιαρβιγάνων, which Chosroes consulted, was a fire worshipped in itself, and sought for oracular purposes.

[3] Zosimus, *Ann.* i. 57.

[4] Macrob. *Sat.* i. 23. Fontenelle's criticism (*Histoire des Oracles*) on the answer given to Trajan is worth reading along with the passage of Macrobius as an example of Voltairian mockery, equally incisive and unjust. Cf. Amm. Marcell. xiv. 7 for a variety of this form of response.

which were spelt out for them by some automatic agency, after a fashion which, from the description of Ammianus we cannot precisely determine.[1] This oracle, construed into a menace against a Christian Emperor, gave rise to a persecution of paganism of so severe a character that, inasmuch as philosophers were believed especially to affect the forbidden practice, the very repute or aspect of a philosopher, as Sozomen tells us,[2] was enough to bring a man under the notice of the police. This theological rancour will the less surprise us, if we believe with some modern criticism that St. Paul himself, under the pseudonym of Simon Magus, had not escaped the charge, at the hands of a polemical Father, of causing the furniture of his house to move without contact, in obedience to his unholy will.[3]

Finally, to conclude this strange list with an example which may by many minds be considered as typical of the rest, it was in this age that, at the Nymphaeum at Apollonia in Epirus, an Ignis Fatuus[4] gave by its waving approach and recession the re-

---

[1] Amm. Marcell. xxix. 2, and xxxi. 1.

[2] Sozomen. vi. 35.

[3] Pseudo-Clemens, *Homil.* ii. 32. 638, τὰ ἐν οἰκίᾳ σκεύη ὡς αὐτόματα φερόμενα πρὸς ὑπηρεσίαν βλέπεσθαι ποιεῖ. Cf. Renan, *Les Apôtres*, p. 153, note, etc.

[4] There can, I think, be little doubt that such was the true character of the flame which Dio Cassius (xli. 45) describes: πρὸς δὲ τὰς ἐπιχύσεις τῶν ὄμβρων ἐπαύξει καὶ ἐς ὕψος ἐξαίρεται, etc. Maury's explanation (ii. 446) is slightly different. The fluctuations of the flame on Etna (Paus. iii. 23) were an instance of a common volcanic phenomenon.

sponses which a credulous people sought,—except that this Will-o'-the-Wisp, with unexpected diffidence, refused to answer questions which had to do with marriage or with death.

Further examples are not needed to prove what the express statement of Tertullian and others testifies,[1] that the world was still "crowded with oracles" in the first centuries of our era. We must now retrace our steps and inquire with what eyes the post-Socratic philosophers[2] regarded a phenomenon so opposed to ordinary notions of enlightenment or progress.

Plato's theory of inspiration is too vast and far reaching for discussion here. It must be enough to say that, although oracles seemed to him to constitute but a small part of the revelation offered by God to man, he yet maintained to the full their utility, and appeared to assume their truth. In his

---

[1] Tertullian, *de Anima*, 46 : Nam et oraculis hoc genus stipatus est orbis, etc. Cf. Plin. *Hist. Nat.* viii. 29 : Nec non et hodie multifariam ab oraculis medicina petitur. Pliny's oracular remedy for hydrophobia (viii. 42) is not now pharmacopœal.

[2] For a good account of pre-Socratic views on this topic, see Bouché-Leclerq, i. 29. But the fragments of the early sages tantalise even more than they instruct. A genuine page of Pythagoras would here be beyond price. But it is the singular fate of the original *Ipse* of our *Ipse Dixit* that while the fact of his having said anything is proverbially conclusive as to its truth we have no trustworthy means of knowing what he really did say. Later ages depict him as the representative of continuous inward inspiration, —as a spirit linked with the Past, the Future, the Unseen, by a vision which is presence and a commerce which is identity.

ideal polity the oracles of the Delphian god were to possess as high an authority, and to be as frequently consulted, as in conservative Lacedæmon, and the express decision of heaven was to be invoked in matters of practical[1] as well as of ceremonial[2] import.

Aristotle, who possessed, — and no man had a better right to it, — a religion all his own, and to which he never converted anybody, delivered himself on the subject of oracular dreams with all his sagacious ambiguity. "It is neither easy," he said, "to despise such things, nor yet to believe them."[3]

The schools of philosophy which were dominant in Greece after the death of Aristotle occupied themselves only in a secondary way with the question of oracles. The Stoics and Academics were disposed to uphold their validity on conservative principles, utilising them as the most moral part of the old creed, the point from which its junction with philosophy was most easily made. Cicero's treatise on divination contains a summary of the conservative view, and it is to be remarked that Cratippus and other Peripatetics disavowed the grosser forms of divination, and believed only in dreams and in the utterances of inspired frenzy.[4]

---

[1] *Leges*, vi. 914.   [2] *Leges*, v. 428 ; *Epinomis*, 362.

[3] Ar. *Div. per Som.* i. 1. He goes on to suggest that dreams, though not θεόπεμπτα, may be δαιμόνια. Elsewhere he hints that the soul may draw her knowledge of the future from her own true nature, which she resumes in sleep. See reff. ap. Bouché-Leclercq, i. 55.   [4] See Cic. *de Div.* i. 3.

Epicureans and Cynics, on the other hand, felt no such need of maintaining connection with the ancient orthodoxy, and allowed free play to their wit in dealing with the oracular tradition, or even considered it as a duty to disembarrass mankind of this among other superstitions. The sceptic Lucian is perhaps of too purely mocking a temper to allow us to ascribe to him much earnestness of purpose in the amusing burlesques [1] in which he depicts the difficulty which Apollo feels in composing his official hexameters, or his annoyance at being obliged to hurry to his post of inspiration whenever the priestess chooses "to chew the bay-leaf and drink of the sacred spring." [2]

The indignation of Oenomaus, a cynic of Hadrian's age, is of a more genuine character, and there

---

[1] *Jupiter Tragoedus; Bis Accusatus*, etc. I need not remind the reader that such scoffing treatment of oracles does not now appear for the first time. The parodies in Aristophanes hit off the pompous oracular obscurity as happily as Lucian's. A recent German writer, on the other hand (Hoffmann, *Orakelwesen*), maintains, by precept and example, that no style can be more appropriate to serious topics.

[2] *Bis Accusatus*, 2. I may remark that although narcotics are often used to produce abnormal utterance (Lane's *Egyptians*, ii. 33; Maury, ii. 479), this mastication of a laurel-leaf or bay-leaf cannot be considered as more than a symbolical survival of such a practice. See, however, *Proceedings* of the Society for Psychical Research, vol. iv. p. 152, note, for a most remarkable effect of laurel-water on a hysterical subject. The drinking of water (Iambl. *Myst. Aeg.* 72; Anacreon xiii.), or even of blood (Paus. ii. 24), would be equally inoperative for occult purposes; and though Pliny says that the water in Apollo's cave at Colophon shortened the drinker's life (*Hist. Nat.* ii. 106), it is difficult to imagine what natural salt could produce hallucination.

is much sarcastic humour in his account of his own
visit to the oracle of Apollo at Colophon; how the
first response which he obtained might have been
taken at random from a book of elegant extracts,
and had also, to his great disgust, been delivered in
the self-same words to a commercial traveller immediately before him ; how, to his second question,
"Who will teach me wisdom?" the god returned an
answer of almost meaningless imbecility ; and how,
when he finally asked, "Where shall I go now?" the
god told him "to draw a long bow and knock over
untold green-feeding ganders."[1]   "And who in the
world," exclaims the indignant philosopher, "will
inform me what these untold ganders may mean?"

Anecdotes like this may seem to warn us that
our subject is drawing to a close.   And to students
of these declining schools of Greek philosophy, it
may well appear that the Greek spirit had burnt
itself out; that all creeds and all speculations were
being enfeebled into an eclecticism or a scepticism,
both of them equally shallow and unreal.   But this
was not to be.   It was destined that every seed
which the great age of Greece had planted should
germinate and grow; and a school was now to
arise which should take hold, as it were, of the
universe by a forgotten clew, and should give fuller

---

[1] Eus. *Pr. Ev.* v. 23—

ἐκ ταννστρόφοιο λᾶας σφενδόνης ἱεὶς ἀνὴρ
χῆνας ἐναρίζειν βολαῖσιν, ἀσπέτους, ποιηβόρους.

meaning and wider acceptance to some of the most remarkable, though hitherto least noticed, utterances of earlier men. We must go back as far as Hesiod to understand the Neoplatonists.

For it is in Hesiod's celebrated story of the Ages of the World[1] that we find the first Greek conception, obscure though its details be,—of a hierarchy of spiritual beings who fill the unseen world, and can discern and influence our own. The souls of heroes, he says, become happy spirits who dwell aloof from our sorrow; the souls of men of the golden age become good and guardian spirits, who flit over the earth and watch the just and unjust deeds of men; and the souls of men of the silver age become an inferior class of spirits, themselves mortal, yet deserving honour from mankind.[2] The same strain of thought appears in Thales, who defines demons as spiritual existences, heroes, as the souls of men separated from the body.[3] Pythagoras held much the same view, and, as we shall see below, believed that in a certain sense these spirits were occasionally to be seen or felt.[4] Heraclitus held " that all things were full of souls and spirits,"[5] and

[1] Hes. *Opp.* 109, *sqq.*

[2] It is uncertain where Hesiod places the abode of this class of spirits; the MSS. read ἐπιχθόνιοι, Gaisford (with Tzetzes) and Wolff, *de Daemonibus,* ὑποχθόνιοι.

[3] Athenag. *Legat. pro Christo,* 21 ; cf. Plut. *de Plac. Phil.* i. 8.

[4] Porph. *vit. Pyth.* 384 ; reff. ap. Wolff. For obsession, see Pseudo-Zaleucus, ap. Stob. *Flor.* xliv. 20.

[5] Diog. Laert. ix. 6.

Empedocles has described in lines of startling power[1] the wanderings through the universe of a lost and homeless soul. Lastly, Plato, in the *Epinomis*,[2] brings these theories into direct connection with our subject by asserting that some of these spirits can read the minds of living men, and are still liable to be grieved by our wrong-doing,[3] while many of them appear to us in sleep by visions, and are made known by voices and oracles, in our health or sickness, and are about us at our dying hour. Some are even visible occasionally in waking reality, and then again disappear, and cause perplexity by their obscure self-manifestation.[4]

Opinions like these, existing in a corner of the vast structure of Platonic thought, passed, as it seems, for centuries with little notice. Almost as unnoticed was the gradual development of the creed known as Orphic, which seems to have begun with making itself master of the ancient mysteries, and

---

[1] Plut. *de Iside*, 26.

[2] I believe, with Grote, etc., that the *Epinomis* is Plato's ; at any rate it was generally accepted as such in antiquity, which is enough for the present purpose.

[3] *Epinomis*, 361. μετέχοντα δὲ φρονήσεως θαυμαστῆς, ἅτε γένους ὄντα εὐμαθοῦς τε καὶ μνήμονος, γιγνώσκειν μὲν ξύμπασαν τὴν ἡμετέραν αὐτὰ διάνοιαν λέγωμεν, καὶ τόν τε καλὸν ἡμῶν καὶ ἀγαθὸν ἅμα θαυμαστῶς ἀσπάζεσθαι καὶ τὸν σφόδρα κακὸν μισεῖν, ἅτε λύπης μετέχοντα ἤδη, κ.τ.λ.

[4] καὶ τοῦτ᾽ εἶναι τότε μὲν ὁρώμενον ἄλλοτε δὲ ἀποκρυφθὲν ἄδηλον γιγνόμενον, θαῦμα κατ᾽ ἀμυδρὰν ὄψιν παρεχόμενον. The precise meaning of ἀμυδρὰ ὄψις is not clear without further knowledge of the phenomena which Plato had in his mind. Comp. the ἀλαμπῆ καὶ ἀμυδρὰν ζωὴν, ὥσπερ ἀναθυμίασιν, which is all that reincarnated demons can look for (Plut. *de Defect.* 10).

only slowly spread through the profane world its
doctrine that this life is a purgation, that this body
is a sepulchre,[1] and that the Divinity, who sur-
rounds us like an ocean, is the hope and home of
the soul.   But a time came when, under the impulse of a great religious movement, these currents
of belief, which had so long run underground, broke
into sight again in an unlooked-for direction. These
tenets, and many more, were dwelt upon and ex-
panded with new conviction by that remarkable
series of men who furnish to the history of Greek
thought so singular a concluding chapter.   And
no part, perhaps, of the Neoplatonic system shows
more clearly than their treatment of oracles how
profound a change the Greek religion has undergone
beneath all its apparent continuity.   It so happens
that the Neoplatonic philosopher who has written
most on our present subject, was also a man whose
spiritual history affords a striking, perhaps an
unique, epitome of the several stages through which
the faith of Greece had up to that time passed.   A
Syrian of noble descent,[2] powerful intelligence, and

---

[1] See, for instance, Plato, *Crat.* 264. δοκοῦσι μέντοι μοι μάλιστα
θέσθαι οἱ ἀμφὶ Ὀρφέα τοῦτο ὄνομα (σῶμα *quasi* σῆμα) ὡς δίκην
διδούσης τῆς ψυχῆς ὧν δὴ ἕνεκα δίδωσι, κ.τ.λ.

[2] G. Wolff, *Porph. de Phil.* etc., has collected a mass of authorities on Porphyry's life, and has ably discussed the sequence of his
writings. But beyond this tract I have found hardly anything
written on this part of my subject,—on which I have dwelt the
more fully, inasmuch as it seems hitherto to have attracted so little
attention from scholars.

upright character, Porphyry brought to the study
of the Greek religion little that was distinctively
Semitic, unless we so term the ardour of his religious impulses, and his profound conviction that
the one thing needful for man lay in the truest
knowledge attainable as to his relation to the divine.
Educated by Longinus, the last representative of
expiring classicism, the Syrian youth absorbed all,
and probably more than all, his master's faith.
Homer became to him what the Bible was to Luther;
and he spent some years in producing the most perfect edition of the *Iliad* and *Odyssey* which had yet
appeared, in order that no fragment of the inspired
text might fail to render its full meaning.   But, as
it seems, in the performance of this task his faith
received the same shock which had been fatal to
the early piety of Greece.   The behaviour of the gods
in Homer was too bad to be condoned.   He discerned, what is probably the truth, that there must
be some explanation of these enormities which is
not visible on the surface, and that nothing short
of some profound mistake could claim acceptance
for such legends as those of Zeus and Kronos, of
Kronos and Uranus, amid so much else that is
majestic and pure.[1]   Many philologists would answer

---

[1] The impossibility of extracting a spiritual religion from
Homer is characteristically expressed by Proclus (*ad. Tim.* 20),
who calls Homer ἀπάθειάν τε νοερὰν καὶ ζωὴν φιλόσοφον οὐχ οἷός τε
παραδοῦναι.

now that the mistake, the disease of language, lay
in the expression in terms of human appetite and
passion of the impersonal sequences of the great
phenomena of Nature; that the most monstrous
tales of mythology mean nothing worse or more
surprising than that day follows night, and night
again succeeds to day.   To Porphyry such explanations were of course impossible.   In default of
Sanskrit he betook himself to allegory.   The truth
which must be somewhere in Homer, but which
plainly was not in the natural sense of the words,
must therefore be discoverable in a non-natural
sense.   The cave of the nymphs, for instance, which
Homer describes as in Ithaca, is not in Ithaca.
Homer must, therefore, have meant by the cave
something quite other than a cave; must have
meant, in fact, to signify by its inside the temporary, by its outside the eternal world.   But this
stage in Porphyry's development was not of long
duration.   As his conscience had revolted from Homer
taken literally, so his intelligence revolted from
such a fashion of interpretation as this.   But yet
he was not prepared to abandon the Greek religion.   That religion, he thought, must possess some
authority, some sacred book, some standard of faith,
capable of being brought into harmony with the
philosophy which, equally with the religion itself,
was the tradition and inheritance of the race.   And
such a rule of faith, if to be found anywhere, must

be found in the direct communications of the gods to men. Scattered and fragmentary though these were, it must be possible to extract from them a consistent system.[1] This is what he endeavoured to do in his work, *On the Philosophy to be drawn from Oracles*, a book of which large fragments remain to us imbedded in Eusebius' treatise *On the Preparation for the Gospel*.

Perhaps the best guarantee of the good faith in which Porphyry undertook this task lies in the fact that he afterwards recognised that he had been unsuccessful. He acknowledged, in terms on which his antagonist Eusebius has gladly seized, that the mystery as to the authors of the responses was too profound, the responses themselves were too unsatisfactory, to admit of the construction from them of a definite and lofty faith. Yet there is one point on which, though his inferences undergo much modification, his testimony remains practically the same.[2] This testimony, based, as he implies and his biographers assert, on personal experience,[3] is mainly concerned with the phenomena of possession or inspiration by an unseen power. These phenomena,

---

[1] ὡς ἂν ἐκ μόνου βεβαίου τὰς ἐλπίδας τοῦ σωθῆναι ἀρυόμενος (Eus. *Pr. Ev.* iv. 6) is the strong expression which Porphyry gives to his sense of the importance of this inquiry.

[2] There is one sentence in the epistle to Anebo which would suggest a contrary view, but the later *De Abstinentia*, etc., seem to me to justify the statement in the text.

[3] See, for instance, Eus. *Pr. Ev.* iv. 6: μάλιστα γὰρ φιλοσόφων οὗτος τῶν καθ' ἡμᾶς δοκεῖ καὶ δαίμοσι καὶ οἷς φησι θεοῖς ὡμιληκέναι.

so deeply involved in the conception of oracles, and which we must now discuss, are familiar to the ethnologist in almost every region of the globe. The savage, readily investing any unusual or striking object in nature with a spirit of its own, is likely to suppose further that a spirit's temporary presence may be the cause of any unusual act or condition of a human being. Even so slight an abnormality as the act of sneezing has generally been held to indicate the operation or the invasion of a god. And when we come to graver departures from ordinary well-being—nightmare, consumption, epilepsy, or madness—the notion that a disease-spirit has entered the sufferer becomes more and more obvious. Ravings which possess no applicability to surrounding facts are naturally held to be the utterances of some remote intelligence. Such ravings, when they have once become an object of reverence, may be artificially reproduced by drugs or other stimuli, and we may thus arrive at the belief in inspiration by an easy road.[1]

There are traces in Greece of something of this reverence for disease, but they are faint and few; and the Greek ideal of soundness in mind and body, the Greek reverence for beauty and strength, seem to have characterised the race from a very early

---

[1] On this subject see *Prim. Cult.* chap. xiv.; Lubbock, *Origin of Civilisation*, pp. 252-5, etc. The Homeric phrase στυγερὸς δέ οἱ ἔχραε δαίμων (*Od.* v. 396) seems to be the Greek expression which comes nearest to the doctrine of disease-spirits.

period.   It is possible indeed that the first tradition of

> " Blind Thamyris and blind Mæonides,
> And Teiresias and Phineus, prophets old,"

may have represented a primitive idea that the
" celestial light shone inward " when the orbs of
vision were darkened.   But the legends which have
reached us scarcely connect Homer's blindness with
his song, and ascribe the three prophets' loss of
sight to their own vanity or imprudence.   In
nymph-possession, which, in spite of Pausanias'
statement, is perhaps an older phenomenon than
Apolline possession, we find delirium honoured, but
it is a delirium proceeding rather from the inhala-
tion of noxious vapours than from actual disease.[1]
And in the choice of the Pythian priestess—while
we find that care is taken that no complication shall
be introduced into the process of oracular inquiry
by her youth or good looks,[2]—there is little evidence to show that any preference was given to
epileptics.[3]   Still less can we trace any such reason

---

[1] See Maury, ii. 475.   Nymph-oracles were especially common
in Bœotia, where there were many caves and springs.—Paus. ix.
2, etc.   The passage from Hippocrates, *De Morbo Sacro*, cited by
Maury, ii. 470, is interesting from its precise parallelism with
savage beliefs, but cannot be pressed as an authority for primitive
tradition.

[2] Diod. Sic. xvi. 27.

[3] Maury (ii. 514) cites Plut. *de Defect. orac.* 46, and *Schol. Ar.
Plut.* 39, in defence of the view that a hysterical subject was chosen
as Pythia.   But Plutarch expressly says (*de Defect.* 50) that it was
necessary that the Pythia should be free from perturbation when

of choice in other oracular sanctuaries. We find
here, in fact, the same uncertainty which hangs over
the principle of selection of the god's mouthpiece
in other shahmanistic countries, where the medicine-
man or angekok is sometimes described as haggard
and nervous, sometimes as in no way distinguish-
able from his less gifted neighbours.

Nor, on the other hand, do we find in Greece
much trace of that other kind of possession of which
the Hebrew prophets are our great example, where
a peculiar loftiness of mind and character seem to
point the prophet out as a fitting exponent of the
will of heaven, and a sudden impulse gives vent in
words, almost unconscious, to thoughts which seem
no less than divine. The majestic picture of Amphiaraus in the Seven against Thebes, the tragic
personality of Cassandra in the Agamemnon, are
the nearest parallels which Greece offers to an
Elijah or a Jeremiah.[1] These, however, are mythi-

---

called on to prophesy, and the Scholion on Aristophanes is equally
indecent and unphysiological. Moreover, Plutarch speaks of the
custom of pouring cold water over the priestess in order to ascer-
tain by her healthy way of shuddering that she was sound in body
and mind. This same test was applied to goats, etc., when about
to be sacrificed. There is no doubt evidence (cf. Maury, ii. 461)
that the faculty of divination was supposed to be hereditary in
certain families (perhaps even in certain localities, Herod. i. 78),
but I cannot find that members of such families were sought for as
priests in oracular seats.

[1] The exclamation of Helen (*Od.* xv. 172)—

κλῦτέ μευ, αὐτὰρ ἐγὼ μαντεύσομαι, ὡς ἐνὶ θυμῷ
ἀθάνατοι βάλλουσι καὶ ὡς τελέεσθαι ὀΐω—

cal characters; and so little was the gift of prophecy associated with moral greatness in later days,
that while Plato attributes it to the action of the
divinity, Aristotle feels at liberty to refer it to bile.[1]

It were much to be wished that some systematic discussion of the subject had reached us from
classical times. But none seems to have been composed, at any rate none has come down to us, till
Plutarch's inquiry as to the causes of the general
cessation of oracles in his age.[2] Plutarch's temper
is conservative and orthodox, but we find, nevertheless, that he has begun to doubt whether Apollo is
in every case the inspiring spirit. On the contrary,
he thinks that sometimes this is plainly not the
case, as in one instance where the Pythia, forced to
prophesy while under the possession of a dumb and
evil spirit, went into convulsions and soon afterwards
died. And he recurs to a doctrine, rendered orthodox, as we have already seen, by its appearance in
Hesiod, but little dwelt on in classical times, a doctrine which peoples the invisible world with a hierarchy of spirits of differing character and power.
These spirits, he believes, give oracles, whose cha-

is as it were a naïve introduction to the art of prophecy. Mene-
laus, when appealed to as to the meaning of the portent observed,
is perplexed : the more confident Helen volunteers an explanation,
and impassioned rhetoric melts into inspired prediction.

[1] Plat. *Ion.* 5.—Ar. *Probl.* xxx.—I cannot dwell here on Plat.
Phaedr. 153, and similar passages, which suggest a theory of inspiration which would carry us far beyond the present topic.

[2] Plut. *de Defect. orac. ; de Pyth. ; de EI apud Delphos.*

racter therefore varies with the character and condition of the inspiring spirit; and of this it is hard
to judge except inferentially, since spirits are apt to
assume the names of gods on whom they in some
way depend, though they may by no means resemble
them in character or power. Nay, spirits are not
necessarily immortal, and the death of a resident
spirit may have the effect of closing an oracular
shrine. The death of Pan himself was announced
by a flying voice to Thamus, a sailor, "about the
isles Echinades;" he was told to tell it at Palodes,
and when the ship reached Palodes there was a
dead calm. He cried out that Pan was dead, and
there was a wailing in all the air.[1]

In Plutarch, too, we perceive a growing disposi-
tion to dwell on a class of manifestations of which
we have heard little since Homer's time,—evocations
of the visible spirits of the dead.[2] Certain places,
it seems, were consecrated by immemorial belief to
this solemn ceremony. At Cumae,[3] at Phigalea,[4] at
Heraclea,[5] on the river Acheron, by the lake Aver-

---

[1] This quasi-human character of Pan (Herod. ii. 146 ; Pind. *Fr.*
68 ; Hyg. *Fab.* 224), coupled with the indefinite majesty which his
name suggested, seems to have been very impressive to the later
Greeks. An oracle quoted by Porphyry (ap. Eus. *Pr. Ev.*) εὔχομαι
βροτὸς γεγώς Πανὶ σύμφυτος θεῷ κ.τ.λ., is curiously parallel to some
Christian hymns in its triumphant sense of human kinship with
the divinity.

[2] *Quaest. Rom. ; de Defect. Orac. ; de Ser. Num. Vind.*

[3] Diod. Sic. iv. 22 ; Ephor. ap. Strab. v. 244.

[4] Paus. iii. 17.   [5] Plut. *Cim.* 6.

nus,[1] men strove to recall for a moment the souls who had passed away, sometimes, as Periander sought Melissa,[2] in need of the accustomed wifely counsel; sometimes, as Pausanias sought Cleonice,[3] goaded by passionate remorse; or sometimes with no care to question, with no need to confess or to be forgiven, but as, in one form of the legend, Orpheus sought Eurydice,[4] travelling to the Thesprotian Aornus, in the hope that her spirit would rise and look on him once again, and waiting for one who came not, and dying in a vain appeal.

But on such stories as these Plutarch will not dogmatically judge; he remarks only, and the remark was more novel then than now, that we know as yet no limit to the communications of soul with soul.

This transitional position of Plutarch may prepare us for the still wider divergence from ancient orthodoxy which we find in Porphyry. Porphyry is indeed anxious to claim for oracular utterances as high an authority as possible; and he continues to ascribe many of them to Apollo himself. But he no longer restricts the phenomena of possession and inspiration within the traditional limits as regards either their time, their place, or their author. He maintains that these phenomena may be reproduced

---

[1] Liv. xxiv. 12, etc. The origin of this νεκυομαντεῖον was probably Greek. See reff. ap. Maury, ii. 467.

[2] Diod. iv. 22; Herod. v. 92, gives a rather different story.

[3] Plut. *Cim.* 6. Paus. iii. 17.   [4] Paus. ix. 30.

according to certain rules at almost any place and time, and that the spirits who cause them are of very multifarious character. I shall give his view at some length, as it forms by far the most careful inquiry into the nature of Greek oracles which has come down to us from an age in which they existed still; and it happens also that while the grace of Plutarch's style has made his essays on the same subject familiar to all, the post-classical date and style of Porphyry and Eusebius have prevented their more serious treatises from attracting much attention from English scholars.

According to Porphyry, then, the oracular or communicating demon or spirit,—we must adopt spirit as the word of wider meaning,—manifests himself in several ways. Sometimes he speaks through the mouth of the entranced " recipient,"[1] sometimes he shows himself in an immaterial, or even in a material form, apparently according to his own rank in the invisible world.[2] The recipient

---

[1] δοχεύς, from δέχομαι, is the word generally used for the human intermediary between the god or spirit and the inquirers. See Lob. *Agl.* p. 108, on the corresponding word καταβολικός for the spirit who is thus received for a time into a human being's organism. Cf. also Firmicus Maternus *De errore prof. relig.* 13 : "Serapis vocatus et intra corpus hominis conlatus talia respondit ;" and the phrase ἐγκατοχήσας τῷ Σαράπιδι (*Inscr. Smyrn.* 3163, ap. Wolff, *de Nov.*)

[2] Porphyry calls these inferior spirits δαιμόνια ὑλικά, and Proclus (*ad Tim.* 142) defines the distinction thus : τῶν δαιμόνων οἱ μὲν ἐν τῇ συστάσει πλέον τὸ πύριον ἔχοντες ὁρατοὶ ὄντες οὐδὲν ἔχουσιν ἀντιτύπως, οἱ δὲ καὶ γῆς μετειληφότες ὑποπίπτουσι τῇ ἀφῇ. It is only the spirits

falls into a state of trance, mixed sometimes with exhausting agitation or struggle,[1] as in the case of the Pythia. And the importance attached to a right choice of time and circumstances for the induction of this trance reminds us of Plutarch's story, already mentioned, of the death of a Pythian priestess compelled to prophesy when possessed by an evil spirit. Another inconvenience in choosing a wrong time seems to have been that false answers were then given by the spirit, who, however, would warn the auditors that he could not give information,[2] or even that he would certainly tell falsehoods,[3] on that particular occasion. Porphyry attributes this occasional falsity to some defect in the surrounding conditions,[4] which confuses the spirit, and prevents him from speaking truly. For on descending into our atmosphere the spirits become subject to the laws and influences which rule mankind, and

who partake of earthly nature who are capable of being touched. These spirits may be of a rank inferior to mankind; Proclus, *ad Tim.* 24, calls them ψυχὰς ἀποτύχουσας μὲν τοῦ ἀνθρωπικοῦ νοῦ, πρὸς δὲ τὰ ζῷα ἐχούσας διάθεσιν.

[1] οὐ φέρει με τοῦ δοχῆος ἡ τάλαινα καρδία (Procl. *ad Rempublicam*, 380) is the exclamation of a spirit whose recipient can no longer sustain his presence.

[2] Eus. *Pr. Ev.* vi. 5, σήμερον οὐκ ἐπέοικε λέγειν ἀστρων ὁδὸι ἱρήν.

[3] *Ibid.* κλεῖε βίην κάρτος τε λόγων· ψευδήγορα λέξω: "Try no longer to enchain me with your words; I shall tell you falsehoods."

[4] ἡ κατάστασις τοῦ περιέχοντος. Eus. *Pr. Ev.* iv. 5, καὶ τὸ περιέχον ἀναγκάζον ψευδῆ γίνεσθαι τὰ μαντεῖα, οὐ τοὺς παρόντας ἑκόντας προστιθέναι τὸ ψεῦδος. . . . πέφηνεν ἄρα, adds Porphyry with satisfaction, πόθεν πολλάκις τὸ ψεῦδος συνίσταται.

are not therefore entirely free agents.[1] When a confusion of this kind occurs, the prudent inquirer should defer his researches,—a rule with which inexperienced investigators fail to comply.[2]

Let us suppose, however, that a favourable day has been secured, and also, not less important, a "guileless intermediary."[3] Some confined space would then be selected for the expected manifestations, "so that the influence should not be too widely diffused."[4] This place seems sometimes to have been made dark,—a circumstance which has not escaped the satire of the Christian controversialist,[5] whose derision is still further excited by the "barbarous yells and singing "[6] with which the unseen visitant was allured,—a characteristic, it may be noticed in passing, of shahmanistic practices, wherever they have been found to prevail. During these proceedings the human agent appears to have

---

[1] Porph. ap. Philoponum, *de Mundi Creat.* iv. 20, with the comments of Philoponus, whose main objection to these theories lies in their interference with the freedom of the will.

[2] *Pr. Ev.* vi. 5, οἱ δὲ μένουσι καὶ λέγειν ἀναγκάζουσι διὰ τὴν ἀμαθίαν.

[3] *Ibid.* v. 8, κάππεσεν ἀμφὶ κάρηνον ἀμωμήτοιο δοχῆος.

[4] καὶ ἅμα ἀποστηρίζοντες αὐτὸ ἐνταῦθα ἔν τινι στερέῳ χωρίῳ ὥστε μὴ ἐπιπολὺ διαχεῖσθαι, Iamb. *de Myst.* iii. 14. The maxims of Iamblichus in these matters are in complete conformity with those of Porphyry.

[5] Eus. *Pr. Ev.* iv. 1, καὶ τὸ σκότος δὲ οὐ μικρὰ συνεργεῖν τῇ καθ' ἑαυτοὺς ὑποθέσει.

[6] *Ibid.* v. 12, ἀσήμοις τε καὶ βαρβάροις ἤχοις τε καὶ φωναῖς κηλούμενοι.

fallen into an abnormal slumber, which extinguished
for the time his own identity, and allowed the spirit
to speak through his lips,—"to contrive a voice for
himself through a mortal instrument."[1]   In such
speeches, of which several are preserved to us, the
informing spirit alludes to the human being through
whom he is speaking in the third person, as "the
mortal" or "the recipient;" of himself he speaks in
the first person, or occasionally in the third person,
as "the god" or "the king."[2]

The controlling spirits do not, however, always
content themselves with this vicarious utterance.
They appear sometimes, as already indicated, in
visible and tangible form.   Of this phase of the
proceedings, however, Eusebius has preserved to us
but scanty notices.   His mind is preoccupied with
the presumption and *bizarrerie* of the spirits, who
sometimes profess themselves to be (for instance)
the sun and moon; sometimes insist on being called
by barbarous names, and talking a barbarous jargon.[3]
The precise nature of such appearances had been, it
seems, in dispute since the days of Pythagoras, who
conjectured that the apparition was an emanation from
the spirit, but not, strictly speaking, the spirit itself.[4]

---

[1] *Ibid.* v. 8 αὐλοῦ δ' ἐκ βροτέοιο φίλην ἐτεκνώσατο φωνήν.

[2] φῶς, βροτός, δοχεύς.   *Pr. Ev.* v. 9, λύετε λοιπὸν ἄνακτα, βροτὸς
θεὸν οὐκέτι χωρεῖ.

[3] *Pr. Ev.* v. 10 (quoting Porph. *ad Aneb.*), τί δὲ καὶ τὰ ἄσημα
βούλεται ὀνόματα καὶ τῶν ἀσήμων τὰ βάρβαρα πρὸ τῶν ἑκάστῳ
οἰκείων, etc.

[4] Pythag. ap. Aen. Gaz. ap. Theophr. p. 61, Boisson.   πότερον

In the Neoplatonic view, these spirits entered by a process of "introduction"[1] into a material body temporarily prepared for them; or sometimes it was said that "the pure flame was compressed into a sacred Form."[2] Those spirits who had already been accustomed to appear were best instructed as to how to appear again; but some of them were inclined to mischief, especially if the persons present showed a careless temper.[3]

Θεοὶ ἢ δαίμονες ἢ τούτων ἀπόρροιαι, καὶ πότερον δαίμων εἰς ἄλλος εἶναι δοκῶν ἢ πολλοὶ καὶ σφῶν αὐτῶν διαφέροντες, οἱ μὲν ἥμεροι, οἱ δ' ἄγριοι, καὶ οἱ μὲν ἐνίοτε τἀληθῆ λέγοντες οἱ δ' ὅλως κίβδηλοι . . . . τέλος προΐεται δαίμονος ἀπόρροιαν εἶναι τὸ φάσμα.

[1] εἴσκρισις. See Lob. Agl. p. 730.

[2] Pr. Ev. v. 8 :—   ἱεροῖσι τύποις
συνθλιβομένου πυρὸς ἁγνοῦ.

I may just notice here the connection between this idea of the entrance of a spirit into a quasi-human form built up for the occasion, and that recrudescence of idol-worship which marks one phase of Neoplatonism.   In an age when such primitive practices as "carrying the dried corpse of a parent round the fields that he might see the state of the crops" (Spencer's *Sociology*, § 154), were no longer possible, this new method of giving temporary materiality to disembodied intelligences suggested afresh that it might be practicable so to prepare an image as that a spirit would be content to live there permanently.   An oracle in Pausanias (ix. 38) curiously illustrates this view of statues.   The land of the Orchomenians was infested by a spirit which sat on a stone.   The Pythia ordered them to make a brazen image of the spectre and fasten it with iron to the stone.   The spirit would still be there, but he would now be permanently fixed down, and, being enclosed in a statue, he would no longer form an obnoxious spectacle.

[3] Pr. Ev. v. 8, ἔθος ποιησάμενοι τῆς ἑαυτῶν παρουσίας εὐμαθέστερον φοιτῶσι καὶ μάλιστα ἐὰν καὶ φύσει ἀγαθοὶ τυγχάνωσιν, οἱ δὲ, κᾂν ἔθος ἔχωσι τοῦ παραγίνεσθαι, βλάβην τινὰ προθυμοῦνται ποιεῖν, καὶ μάλιστα ἐὰν ἀμελέστερόν τις δοκῇ ἀναστρέφεσθαι ἐν τοῖς πράγμασι.   This notion

After a time the spirit becomes anxious to depart; but is not always able to quit the intermediary as promptly as it desires. We possess several oracles uttered under these circumstances, and giving directions which we can but imperfectly understand. It appears that the recipient, for what reason we are left to conjecture, was in some way bound with withes and enveloped in fine linen, which had to be cut and unwrapped at the end of the ceremony.[1] The human agent had then to be set on his feet and taken from the corner where he had been outstretched, and a singular collaboration seems to have taken place, the spirit giving his orders to the bystanders by a voice issuing from the recipient's still senseless form.[2] At last the spirit departs, and the recipient is set free.

Eusebius, in a passage marked by strong common sense,[3] has pointed out some obvious objections to oracles obtained in this fashion. Some of these so-

---

of a congruity between the inquirer and the responding spirit is curiously illustrated by a story of Caracalla (Dio Cass. lxxvii.), who ἐψυχαγώγησε μὲν ἄλλας τέ τινας καὶ τὴν τοῦ πατρὸς τοῦ τε Κομμόδου ψυχήν· εἶτε δ' οὖν οὐδεὶς αὐτῷ οὐδέν, πλὴν τοῦ Κομμόδου. Ἔφη γὰρ ταῦτα· βαῖνε δίκης ἆσσον, θεοὶ ἦν αἰτοῦσι Σεβήρῳ. No ghost would address Caracalla except the ghost of Commodus, who spoke to denounce to him his doom.

[1] Pr. Ev. v. 8:—παύεο δὴ περίφρων ὀάρων, ἀνάπαυε δὲ φῶτα,
θάμνων ἐκλύων πολιὸν τύπον, ἠδ' ἀπὸ γυίων
Νειλαίην ὀθόνην χερσὶν στιβαρῶς ἀπάειρας.
And again, when the bystanders delay the release, the spirit exclaims— σινδόνος ἀμπέτασον νεφέλην, λῦσόν τε δοχῆα.

[2] Pr. Ev. v. 8;—ὑψίπρωρον αἶρε ταρσόν, ἴσχε βάξιν ἐκ μυχῶν. And again, ἄρατε φῶτα γαληθεν ἀναστήσαντες ἑταῖροι, etc.

[3] Pr. Ev. iv. 2.

called "recipients," it appears, had been put to the torture and had made damaging confessions. Further penalties had induced them to explain how their fraud was carried out. The darkness and secrecy of the proceedings were in any case suspicious; and the futility of many of the answers obtained, or their evident adaptation to the wishes of the inquirers, pointed too plainly to their human origin. The actual method of producing certain phenomena has exercised the ingenuity of other Fathers. Thus figures could be shown in a bowl of water by using a moveable bottom, or lights could be made to fly about in a dark room by releasing a vulture with flaming tow tied to its claws.[1]

But in spite of these contemptuous criticisms the Christian Fathers, as is well known, were disposed to believe in the genuineness of some at least of these communications, and showed much anxiety to induce the oracles, which often admitted the greatness and wisdom, to acknowledge also the divinity, of Christ.[2]

Eusebius himself, in another work,[3] adduces a letter of Constantine's describing an oracle said to have been uttered directly by Apollo "from a certain dark hole," in which the god asserted that he could no longer speak the truth on account of

---

[1] Pseudo-Origen, *Philosophumena*, p. 73.

[2] *Pr. Ev.* iv. iii. 7. Aug. *de Civit. Dei*, xix. 23. Lact. *Instit.* iv. 13.

[3] *Vit. Const.* ii. 50; cf. Wolff, *de Noviss.* p. 4.

the number of saints who were now on the earth. But this has so little the air of an Apolline manifestation that it is suspected that a Christian man had crept into a cave and delivered this unauthorised response with a polemical object.[1]

Into so obscure, so undignified a region of mingled fraud and mystery does it seem that, by the admission of friends and foes alike, the oracles of Greece had by this time fallen. Compared with what had been stripped away, that which was left may seem to us like the narrow vault of the Delian sanctuary compared with the ruined glories of that temple-covered isle. There was not, indeed, in Porphyry's view anything inconsistent with the occasional presence and counsel of a lofty and a guardian spirit. There was nothing which need make him doubt that the Greeks had been led upwards through their long history by some providential power. Nay, he himself cites, as we shall see, recent oracles higher in tone than any which have preceded them. Yet as compared with the early ardour of that imaginative belief which peopled heaven with gods and earth with heroes, we feel that we are now sent back to " beggarly elements ;" that the task of sifting truth from falsehood amid so much deception and incompetency on the part both of visible and

---

[1] The well-known story, Γρηγόριος τῷ Σατανᾷ Εἴσελθε—Greg. Nyss. 548 (and to be found in all lives of Gregory Thaumaturgus), illustrates this Christian rivalry with pagan oracles or apparitions.

invisible agencies,[1] of erecting a consistent creed on such mean and shifting foundations, might well rebut even the patient ardour of this most untiring of " seekers after God." And when we see him recognising all this with painful clearness, giving vent, in that letter to Anebo which is so striking an example of absolute candour in an unscrupulous and polemic age, to his despair at the obscurity which seems to deepen as he proceeds, we cannot but wonder that we do not see him turn to take refuge in the new religion with its offers of certainty and peace.

Why, we shall often ask, should men so much in earnest as the Neoplatonists have taken, with the gospel before them, the side they took? Why should they have preferred to infuse another allegory into the old myths which had endured so much? to force the Pythian Apollo, so simple-hearted through all his official ambiguity, to strain his hexameters into the ineffable yearnings of a theosophic age? For we seem to see the issues so clearly! when we take up Augustine instead of Proclus we feel so instantly that we have changed to the winning side! But to Greek minds—and the glory of the Syrian Porphyry was that, of all barbarians, he became the most intensely Greek—the struggle

---

[1] The disappointing falsity of the manifesting spirits who pretended to be the souls of departed friends, etc., is often alluded to ; e.g. in the ad Anebonem : οἱ δὲ εἶναι μὲν ἔξωθεν τίθενται τὸ ὑπήκοον γένος ἀπατηλῆς φύσεως, παντόμορφόν τε καὶ πολύτροπον, ὑποκρινόμενον καὶ θεοὺς καὶ δαίμονας καὶ ψυχὰς τεθνηκότων, etc.

presented itself in a very different fashion. They were fighting not for an effete mythology, but for the whole Past of Greece; nay, as it seemed in a certain sense, for the civilisation of the world. The repulse of Xerxes had stirred in the Greeks the consciousness of their uniqueness as compared with the barbarism on every side. And now, when Hellenism was visibly dying away, there awoke in the remaining Greeks a still more momentous conception, the conception of the uniqueness and preciousness of Greek life not only in space but in duration, as compared not only with its barbarian compeers, but with the probable future of the world. It was no longer against the Great King, but against Time itself, that the unequal battle must be waged. And while Time's impersonal touch was slowly laid upon all the glory which had been, a more personal foe was seen advancing from the same East from whose onset Greece had already escaped, "but so as by fire." Christ, like Xerxes, came against the Greek spirit Συριήγενες ἅρμα διώκων, driving a Syrian car; the tide of conquest was rolling back again, and the East was claiming an empire such as the West had never won.

We, indeed, knowing all the flower of European Christianity in Dante's age, all its ripening fruit in our own, may see that this time from the East light came; we may trust and claim that we are living now among the scattered forerunners of such types of beauty and of goodness as Athens never knew. But if so much even of our own ideal is in the future still, how must it have been to those whose longest outlook could not overpass the dreary centuries of barbarism and decay? So vast a spiritual revolution must needs bring to souls of differing temper very different fates. Happy were they who, like Augustine and Origen, could frankly desert the old things and rejoice that all things were become new. Happy, too, were those few saintly souls—an Antoninus or a Plotinus—whose lofty calm no spiritual revolution seemed able to reach or mar. But the pathetic destiny was that of men like Julian or Porphyry, men who were disqualified from leading the race onward into a noble future merely because they so well knew and loved an only less noble past.

And yet it is not for long that we can take Porphyry as an example of a man wandering in the twilight between "dying lights and dawning," between an outworn and an untried faith. The last chapter in the history of oracles is strangely connected with the last stage of the spiritual history of this upward-striving man.

For it was now that Porphyry was to encounter an influence, a doctrine, an aim, more enchanting than Homer's mythology, profounder than Apollo's oracles, more Christian, I had almost written, than Christianity itself. More Christian at least than such Christianity as had chiefly met Porphyry's eyes; more Christian than the violence of bishops, the wrangles of heretics, the fanaticism of slaves, was that single-hearted and endless effort after the union of the soul with God which filled every moment of the life of Plotinus, and which gave to his living example a potency and a charm which his writings never can renew.[1] "Without father, without mother, without descent," a figure appearing solitary as Melchisedek on the scene of history, charged with a single blessing and lost in the unknown, we may yet see in this chief of mystics the heir of Plato, and affirm that it is he who has completed the cycle of Greek civilisation by adding to that long gallery of types of artist and warrior, philosopher and poet, the stainless image of the saint.

It may be that the holiness which he aimed at is not for man. It may be that ecstasy comes best unsought, and that the still small voice is heard seldomer in the silence of the wilderness than through the thunder of human toil and amid human passion's fire.

But those were days of untried capacities, of unbounded hopes. In the Neoplatonist lecture-

[1] Eunapius (*vit. Porph.*) manages to touch the heart, in spite of his affectations, when he describes the friendship between Porphyry and Plotinus. Of Porphyry's first visit to Rome he says :—τὴν μεγίστην Ῥώμην ἰδεῖν ἐπιθυμήσας . . . ἐπειδὴ τάχιστα εἰς αὐτὴν ἀφίκετο καὶ τῷ μεγίστῳ Πλωτίνῳ συνῆλθεν εἰς ὁμιλίαν, πάντων ἐπελάθετο τῶν ἄλλων, κ.τ.λ.

room, as at the Christian love-feast, it seemed that religion had no need to compromise, that all this complex human spirit could be absorbed and transfigured in one desire.

Counsels of perfection are the aliment of strenuous souls, and henceforth, in each successive book of Porphyry's, we see him rising higher, resting more confidently in those joys and aspirations which are the heritage of all high religions, and the substance of the communion of saints.

And gradually, as he dwells more habitually in the thought of the supreme and ineffable Deity, the idea of a visible or tangible communion with any Being less august becomes repugnant to his mind. For what purpose should he draw to him those unknown intelligences from the ocean of environing souls? "For on those things which he desires to know there is no prophet nor diviner who can declare to him the truth, but himself only, by communion with God, who is enshrined indeed in his heart."[1] "By a sacred silence we do Him honour, and by pure thoughts of what He is."[2] "Holding Him fast, and being made like unto Him, let us present ourselves, a holy sacrifice, for our offering unto God."[3]

---

[1] *De Abstin.* ii. 54.

[2] *Ibid.* ii. 34, διὰ δὲ σιγῆς καθαρᾶς καὶ τῶν περὶ αὐτοῦ καθαρῶν ἐννοιῶν θρησκεύομεν αὐτῷ.

[3] *Ibid.* ii. 34, δεῖ ἄρα συναφθέντας καὶ ὁμοιωθέντας αὐτῷ τὴν αὐτῶν ἀναγωγὴν θυσίαν ἱερὰν προσαγαγεῖν τῷ θεῷ.

And in his letter to the well-loved wife of his
old age,—than which we find no higher expression
of the true Platonic love (so often degraded and
misnamed)—no nobler charge and counsel of man
to woman in all the stores which antiquity has
bequeathed,— in this last utterance we find him
risen above all doubt and controversy, and rapt in
the contemplation of that Being whom " no prayers
can move and no sacrifice honour, nor the abun- .
dance of offerings find favour in His sight; only
the inspired thought fixed firmly on Him has cog-
nisance of God indeed."[1]   It may seem that as we
enter on this region we have left oracles behind.
But it is not so.   The two last oracles which I shall
cite, and which are among the most remarkable of
all, are closely connected with this last period of
Porphyry's life.   The first of them is found, by no
chance we may be sure, on a leaf of the manuscript
which contains his letter to Marcella.   It is introduced to us by an unknown writer as " an oracle
concerning the Eternal God."[2]

[1] τὸ ἔνθεον φρόνημα καλῶς ἡδρασμένον συνάπτεται τῷ θεῷ.—See the
Ad Marcellam passim.

[2] This oracle was very probably actually delivered in a shrine,
as the utterances of this period were often tinged with Neoplatonism.
I have followed Wolff's emendations, and must refer the reader to
his Porph. Fragm. p. 144, and especially his Addit. IV. de Daemonibus, p. 225, in support of the substantial accuracy of my rendering.
It is impossible to reproduce all the theology which this hymn contains ; I have tried to bring out the force of the most central and
weighty expressions, such as ἀενάοις ὀχετοῖσι τιθηνῶν νοῦν ἀτάλαντον.
The oracle will also be found in Steuchus, de Perenni Philosophia,

"O God ineffable, eternal Sire,
Throned on the whirling spheres, the astral fire,
Hid in whose heart thy whole creation lies,—
The whole world's wonder mirrored in thine eyes,—
List thou thy children's voice, who draw anear,
Thou hast begotten us, thou too must hear!
Each life thy life her Fount, her Ocean knows,
Fed while it fosters, filling as it flows;
Wrapt in thy light the star-set cycles roll,
And worlds within thee stir into a soul;
But stars and souls shall keep their watch and way,
Nor change the going of thy lonely day.
　　Some sons of thine, our Father, King of kings,
Rest in the sheen and shelter of thy wings,—
Some to strange hearts the unspoken message bear,
Sped on thy strength through the haunts and homes of
　　air,—
Some where thine honour dwelleth hope and wait,
Sigh for thy courts and gather at thy gate;
These from afar to thee their praises bring,
Of thee, albeit they have not seen thee, sing;
Of thee the Father wise, the Mother mild,
Thee in all children the eternal Child,
Thee the first Number and harmonious Whole,
Form in all forms, and of all souls the Soul."

The second oracle above alluded to, the last which
I shall quote, was given, as Porphyry tells us, at
Delphi to his friend Amelius, who inquired, "Where
was now Plotinus' soul?"[1]

iii. 14 ; Orelli, *Opusc. gr. vett. sentent.* i. 319; and Mai's edition of
the *Ad Marcellam.*
　　[1] Porph. *vit. Plot.* 22.　It is seldom that the genuineness of an

Whatever be the source of this poem, it stands
out to us as one of the most earnest utterances of
antiquity, though it has little of classical perfection
of form.   Nowhere, indeed, is the contest more
apparent between the intensity of the emotions which
are struggling for utterance and the narrow limits
of human speech, which was composed to deal with
the things that are known and visible, and not with
those that are inconceivable and unseen.

Little, in truth, it is which the author of this
oracle could express, less which the translator can
render; but there is enough to show once more the
potency of an elect soul, what a train of light she
may leave behind her as she departs on her unknown
way; when for those who have lived in her presence,
but can scarcely mourn her translation, the rapture
of love fades into the rapture of worship.   Plotinus
was "the eagle soaring above the tomb of Plato;"
no wonder that the eyes which followed his flight
must soon be blinded with the sun.

> " Pure spirit—once a man—pure spirits now
>   Greet thee rejoicing, and of these art thou;

oracle can be established on grounds which would satisfy the critical
historian.   But this oracle has better external evidence than most
others.   Of Porphyry's own good faith there is no question, and
though we know less of the character of his fellow-philosopher
Amelius, it seems unlikely that he would have wished to deceive
Porphyry on an occasion so solemn as the death of their beloved
master, or even that he could have deceived him as to so considerable an undertaking as a journey to Delphi.

Not vainly was thy whole soul alway bent
With one same battle and one the same intent
Through eddying cloud and earth's bewildering roar
To win her bright way to that stainless shore.
Ay, 'mid the salt spume of this troublous sea,
This death in life, this sick perplexity,
Oft on thy struggle through the obscure unrest
A revelation opened from the Blest—
Showed close at hand the goal thy hope would win,
Heaven's kingdom round thee and thy God within.[1]
So sure a help the eternal Guardians gave,
From life's confusion so were strong to save,
Upheld thy wandering steps that sought the day
And set them steadfast on the heavenly way.
Nor quite even here on thy broad brows was shed
The sleep which shrouds the living, who are dead;
Once by God's grace was from thine eyes unfurled
This veil that screens the immense and whirling world,
Once, while the spheres around thee in music ran,
Was very Beauty manifest to man;—
Ah, once to have seen her, once to have known her there,
For speech too sweet, for earth too heavenly fair!
But now the tomb where long thy soul had lain
Bursts, and thy tabernacle is rent in twain;
Now from about thee, in thy new home above,
Has perished all but life, and all but love,—
And on all lives and on all loves outpoured
Free grace and full, a Spirit from the Lord,

---

[1] ἐφάνη γοῦν τῷ Πλωτίνῳ σκοπὸς ἐγγύθι ναίων· τέλος γὰρ αὐτῷ καὶ σκοπὸς ἦν τὸ ἐνωθῆναι καὶ πελάσαι τῷ ἐπὶ πᾶσι θεῷ. Ἔτυχε δὲ τετράκις που, ὅτε συνήμην αὐτῷ, τοῦ σκοποῦ τούτου ἐνεργείᾳ ἀρρήτῳ καὶ οὐ δυνάμει.—(Porph. vit. Plot.)

High in that heaven whose windless vaults enfold
Just men made perfect, and an age all gold.
Thine own Pythagoras is with thee there,
And sacred Plato in that sacred air,
And whoso followed, and all high hearts that knew
In death's despite what deathless Love can do.
To God's right hand they have scaled the starry way—
Pure spirits these, thy spirit pure as they.
Ah saint! how many and many an anguish past,
To how fair haven art thou come at last!
On thy meek head what Powers their blessing pour,
Filled full with life, and rich for evermore!"

This, so far as we know, was the last utterance
of the Pythian priestess. Once more, indeed, a
century afterwards, a voice was heard at Delphi.
But that voice seems rather to have been, in
Plutarch's phrase, "a cry floating of itself over
solitary places," than the deliverance of any recognised priestess, or from any abiding shrine. For
no shrine was standing more. The words which
answered the Emperor Julian's search were but the
whisper of desolation, the last and loveliest expression of a sanctity that had passed away. A strange
coincidence! that from that Delphian valley, whence,
as the legend ran, had sounded the first of all hexameters,[1]—the call, as in the childhood of the world,
to "birds to bring their feathers and bees their
wax" to build by Castaly the nest-like habitation

---

[1] ξυμφέρετε πτερά τ' οἰωνοὶ κηρόν τε μέλιτται.—Plut. de Pyth.
xvii.; and reff. ap. Hendess, Orac. Graec. p. 36.

of the young new-entering god, — from that same
ruined place where " to earth had fallen the glorious
dwelling," from the dry channel where " the water-
springs that spake were quenched and dead,"—
should issue in unknown fashion the last fragment
of Greek poetry which has moved the hearts of
men, the last Greek hexameters which retain the
ancient cadence, the majestic melancholy flow ! [1]

Stranger still, and of deeper meaning, is the fate
which has ordained that Delphi, born with the
birth of Greece, symbolising in her teaching such
light and truth as the ancient world might know,
silenced once only in her long career, and silenced
not by Christ, but by Antichrist, should have proclaimed in her last triumphant oracle the canonisa-
tion of the last of the Greeks, should have responded
with her last sigh and echo to the appeal of the
last of the Romans.

And here I shall leave the story of Greek
oracles. It may be, indeed, that some strange and
solitary divinities—the god Jaribolus at Palmyra,[2]
the god Marnas at Gaza,[3] the god Besa at

----

[1] εἴπατε τῷ βασιλῆι, χαμαὶ πέσε δαίδαλος αὐλά·
    οὐκέτι Φοῖβος ἔχει καλύβαν, οὐ μάντιδα δάφνην,
    οὐ παγὰν λαλέουσαν· ἀπέσβετο καὶ λάλον ὕδωρ.
—Ge. Cedren. *Hist. Comp.* i. 304 ; and see Mr. Swinburne's poem,
"The Last Oracle."

[2] *Inscr. Gr.* 4483 ap. Wolff, *de Noviss.* p. 27. There is, however, no proof of Jaribolian utterance later than A.D. 242.

[3] Marc. Diac. *vit. Porph. Episc.* ap. *Acta Sanctorum,* and Wolff,
de Noviss. p. 26. Circ. A.D. 400.

Abydos[1]—still uttered from time to time some perishing prophecy, some despairing protest against the new victorious faith.   But that such oracles there still were is proved rather from Christian legislation than from heathen records.   On these laws I will not dwell, nor recount how far the Christian emperors fell from their divine ideal when they punished by pillage,[2] by torture,[3] and by death[4] the poor unlearned "villagers," whose only crime it was that they still found in the faith of their fathers the substance of things hoped for, and an evidence of things not seen.   Such stains will mar the noblest revolutions, but must not blind us to the fact that a spiritual revolution follows only on a spiritual need.   The end of the Greek oracles was determined not from without, but from within. They had passed through all their stages.   Fetishism, Shahmanism, Nature-worship, Polytheism, even Monotheism and Mysticism, had found in turn a home in their immemorial shrines.   Their utterances had reflected every method in which man has

---

[1] Amm. Marc. xix. 12 (A.D. 359).

[2] *Cod. Theod.* xvi. 10 (Theodosius I.)

[3] Amm. Marc. xxi. 12 (Constantius).

[4] *Cod. Justin.* ix. 18 (Constantius) ; *Theod. leg. Novell.* iii. (Theodosius II.)   These laws identify paganism as far as possible with magic, and, by a singular inversion, Augustine quotes Virgil's authority (*Aen.* iv. 492) in defence of the persecution of his own faith.   See Maury, *Magie,* etc., p. 127.   The last struggle of expiring paganism was in defence of the oracular temple of Serapis at Alexandria, A.D. 389

sought communion with the Unseen, from systematic experiment to intuitive ecstasy. They had completed the cycle of their scripture from its Theogony to its Apocalypse; it was time that a stronger wave of revelation should roll over the world, and that what was best and truest in the old religion should be absorbed into and identified with the new.[1]

And if there be some who feel that the youth, the *naïveté*, the unquestioning conviction, must perish not from one religion only, but from all; that the more truly we conceive of God, the more unimaginable He becomes to us, and the more infinite, and the more withdrawn; that we can no longer "commune with Him from oak or rock as a young man communes with a maid;"—to such men the story of the many pathways by which mankind has striven to become cognisant of the Unseen may have an aspect of hope as well as of despondency.

For before we despair of a question as unanswerable we must know that it has been rightly asked. And there are problems which can become clearly

[1] I need hardly remind the reader that the Church continued till the Renaissance to believe in the reality of the Greek oracles, though condemning the "demons" who inspired them. To refer them, in fact, entirely to illusion and imposture is an argument not without danger for the advocate of any revealed religion. "Celui," says M. Bouché-Leclercq, "qui croit à la Providence et à l'efficacité de la prière doit se rappeler qu'il accepte tous les principes sur lesquels repose la divination antique."

defined to us only by the aid of premature and imperfect solutions.   There are many things which
we should never have known had not inquiring
men before us so often deemed vainly that they knew.

Suspense of judgment, indeed, in matters of such
moment, is so irksome an attitude of mind, that we
need not wonder if confidence of view on the one
side is met by a corresponding confidence on the
other; if the trust felt by the mass of mankind in
the adequacy of one or other of the answers to these
problems which have been already obtained is re-
butted by the decisive assertion that all these
answers have been proved futile and that it is idle
to look for more.

Yet such was not the temper of those among
the Greeks who felt, as profoundly perhaps as we,
the darkness and the mystery of human fates.   To
them it seemed no useless or unworthy thing to
ponder on these chief concerns of man with that
patient earnestness which has unlocked so many
problems whose solution once seemed destined to
be for ever unknown.   "For thus will God," as
Sophocles says in one of those passages (*Fr.* 707)
whose high serenity seems to answer our perplexities
as well as his own—

> " Thus then will God to wise men riddling show
>   Such hidden lore as not the wise can know ;
>   Fools in a moment deem his meaning plain,
>   His lessons lightly learn, and learn in vain."

And even now, in the face of philosophies of materialism and of negation so far more powerful than any which Sophocles had to meet, there are yet some minds into which, after all, a doubt may steal,—whether we have indeed so fully explained away the beliefs of the world's past, whether we can indeed so assuredly define the beliefs of its future,—or whether it may not still befit us to track with fresh feet the ancient mazes, to renew the world-old desire, and to set no despairing limit to the knowledge or the hopes of man.

"Light among the vanished ages; star that gildest yet this
    phantom shore ;
Golden branch amid the shadows, kings and realms that set to
    rise no more."

In literature, as in life, affection and reverence may reach a point which disposes to silence rather than to praise. The same ardour of worship which prompts to missions or to martyrdom when a saving knowledge of the beloved object can be communicated so, will shrink from all public expression when the beauty which it reveres is such as can be made manifest to each man only from within. A sense of desecration mingles with the sense of incapacity in describing what is so mysterious, so glorious, and so dear.

Perhaps the admirer may hear the object of his reverence ignorantly misapprehended, unwisely judged. Still he will shrink from speech; he will be unwilling to seem to proffer his own poor and disputable opinion on matters which lie so far above any support which he can give. Yet, possibly, if his admiration has notoriously been shared for nineteen centuries by all whose admiration was best worth having, he may venture to attempt to prove the world right where others have attempted the bolder task of proving it mistaken; or rather, if the matter in question be one by its very nature incapable of proof, he may without presumption restate in terms adapted to modern readers the traditional judgment of sixty generations of men.[1]

The set which the German criticism of this century has made against Virgil is a perfectly explicable, and in one sense a perfectly justifiable thing. It is one among many results which have followed from the application of the historical faculty, pure and simple, to the judgment of Art. Since every work of art is a historical product, it can be used to illus-

---

[1] In writing on an author who has been so constantly discussed for many centuries it is impossible to refer each fragment of criticism to its original source. Most of the sounder reflections on Virgil have occurred to many minds and long ago, and form an anonymous—almost an œcumenical—tradition. Among modern writers on Virgil, I have consulted Bernhardy, Boissier, Cantù, Comparetti, Conington, Gladstone, Henry, Heyne, Keble, Long, Nettleship, Ribbeck, Sainte-Beuve, Sellar, Teuffel, Wagner, etc. ; some of them with mere dissent and surprise, others—especially Boissier and Conington—with great interest and profit. But next to Virgil's own poems, I think that the Divina Commedia is the most important aid to his right apprehension. The exquisite truth and delicacy of Dante's conception of his great master become more and more apparent if the works of the two are studied in connection.

Since this essay was first published, the greatest poet of our times has offered to Virgil a crowning homage,—in accents that recall his own.

trate the growth of the national life from which it
springs; it can be represented as the necessary
result of its epoch and its environment. The several
arts, however, offer very different facility to the
scientific historian. Music, the most unmixedly
imaginative of the arts, has baffled all efforts to
correlate her growth with the general march of
society. Painting bears a more intimate relation to
life, and in much of the preference which has been
lately shown for early *naïveté* over self-conscious
excellence we may detect a mixture of the historical
with the purely æsthetic instinct. The historic
instinct, indeed, works in admirably with the tastes
of an elaborate civilisation. For the impulse of
historic science is naturally towards the Origines or
sources of things; it seeks to track styles and
processes to their fountain-head, and to find them
exhibiting themselves without self-consciousness
or foreign admixture; it would even wish to
eliminate the idiosyncrasies of individual artists
from its generalised estimate of the genius of a
nation. And in highly-cultivated societies there is
a somewhat similar craving—a wish to escape from
all that speaks of effort or preparation, into the
refreshing simplicity of a spontaneous age. This
craving was strongly felt under the Roman Empire;
it is potent among ourselves; it is wholly natural
and innocent so long as it is not allowed to sway
us in our estimate of the highest art.

But if the historical spirit can thus modify the
judgments passed upon painting, much more is this
the case with regard to poetry. For poetry is the
most condensed and pregnant of all historical
phenomena; it is a kind of crystallised deposit of
the human spirit. It is most necessary that the
historian and the philologer should be allowed free
range over this rich domain. And there is no
doubt a sense in which poems, as they become more
remote from us, are fuller of the rough reality of
things. There is a sense in which the song of the
Fratres Arvales is of more value than the Fourth
Eclogue. And there is a sense—and this is a
point on which the Germans have especially dwelt
—in which the whole Latin literature of the
Augustan age, whose outer form, at least, is so con-
fessedly derived from Greek models, is of less
interest than those models themselves. If we wish
to understand the native type, the original essence
of epic or lyric poetry, we must go to Homer and
not to Virgil, to Sappho and not to Horace. Yet
this test, like all sweeping and *à priori* methods of
estimating works of art, requires in practice so
many limitations as to be almost valueless. .It is
impossible to judge a literature by its originality
alone, without condemning much that is best in our
modern literatures more severely than we condemn
the Augustan poets. Imitation is very much a
matter of chronology; it may be conscious or un-

conscious,—ostentatious or concealed,—but as the world goes on, it tends irresistibly to form a larger and larger element in all new productions. And yet each new production may be in essentials superior to its type or forerunner. Its relative merit can be determined by experience alone—can only be judged, for instance, in the case of poetry by the uncertain and difficult process of comparing the amount of delight and elevation received from each work by the consensus of duly qualified men. For, in the face of some recent German criticism, it seems important to repeat that in order to judge poetry it is before all things necessary to enjoy it. We may all desire that historical and philological science should push her dominion into every recess of human action and human speech. But we must utter some protest when the very heights of Parnassus are invaded by a spirit which surely is not Science, but her unmeaning shadow;—a spirit which would degrade every masterpiece of human genius into the mere pabulum of hungry professors, and which values a poet's text only as a field for the rivalries of sterile pedantry and arbitrary conjecture.

It is sometimes said, *àpropos* of the new unction with which physical science has assumed the office of the preacher, that men of the world must be preached to either by men of the world or by saints — not by persons, however eminent and right-minded, whose emotions have been confined to the laboratory.   There is something of a similar incongruity in the attitude of a German commentator laboriously endeavouring to throw a new light on some point of delicate feeling or poetic propriety. Thus one of them objects to Dido's " auburn tress " on the ground that a widow's hair should be of a darker colour.   Another questions whether a broken heart can be properly termed " a fresh wound," if a lady has been suffering from it for more than a week.   A third bitterly accuses Virgil of exaggerating the felicity of the Golden Age.   And Ribbeck alters the text of Virgil, in defiance of all the manuscripts, because the poet's picture (A. xii. 55) of Amata, " self-doomed to die, clasping for the last time her impetuous son-in-law," seems to him tame and unsatisfactory.   By the alteration of *moritura* into *monitura* he is able to represent Amata as clinging to Turnus, not " with the intention of killing herself," but " with the intention of giving advice," which he considers as the more impressive and fitting attitude for a mother-in-law.[1]

It seems somewhat doubtful whither this lofty *à priori* road may lead us.   And yet it is impossible to criticise any form of art without the introduction

---

[1] A single instance will give an idea of Ribbeck's fitness to deal with metrical questions. In A. ix. 67, "qua temptet ratione aditus, et quae via clausos," he reads (against all the MSS.) *et qua vi clausos*, and proves at some length the elegance of his trispondaic termination.

of subjective impressions of some kind. It would be in vain to attempt to give any such general exposition of poetical excellence as should carry conviction to all minds. Some obvious shortcomings may be pointed out, some obvious merits insisted on; but when a higher region is reached we find that a susceptibility to the specific power of poetry is no more communicable than an ear for music. To most readers the subtle, the unexpressed, the infinite element in poetry such as Virgil's will remain for ever unacknowledged and unknown. Like the golden bough which unlocked the secrets of the underworld—

"Itself will follow, and scarce thy touch await,
    If thou be chosen, and if this be fate;
    Else for no force shalt thou its coming feel,
    Nor shear it from the stem with shattering steel."[1]

---

[1] A. vi. 146. The translations from Virgil which I have given in this essay, though faithful to his meaning, as I apprehend it, are not verbally exact; while, like all my predecessors, I have failed to convey any adequate notion of his music or his dignity, and may well fear the fate of Salmoneus, "who thought to rival with flash of lamps and tramp of horses the inimitable thunderbolt and storm." But to reproduce a great poet in another language is as impossible as to reproduce Nature on canvas; and the same controversy between a literal and an impressional rendering divides landscape-painters and translators of poetry. In the case of an author so complex and profound as Virgil, every student will naturally discern a different phase of his significance, and it seems almost a necessary element in any attempt to criticise him that the critic should try to show the view which he takes of a few well-known passages. Mr. Morris' brilliant and accurate version

A few general considerations, however, may at
any rate serve to indicate the kinds of achievement at which Virgil aimed — the kinds of merit
which are or are not to be looked for in his poems.

The range of human thoughts and emotions
greatly transcends the range of such symbols as
man has invented to express them; and it becomes
therefore, the business of Art to use these symbols
in a double way.   They must be used for the direct
representation of thought and feeling; but they
must also be combined by so subtle an imagination
as to suggest much which there is no means of
directly expressing.   And this can be done; for
experience shows that it is possible so to arrange
forms, colours, and sounds as to stimulate the
imagination in a new and inexplicable way.   This
power makes the painter's art an imaginative as
well as an imitative one; and gives birth to the
art of the musician, whose symbols are hardly imitative at all, but express emotions which, till music
suggests them, have been not only unknown but
unimaginable.   Poetry is both an imitative and an
imaginative art.   As a choice and condensed form
of emotional speech, it possesses the reality which depends on its directly recalling our previous thoughts
and feelings.   But as a system of rhythmical and
melodious effects — not indebted for their potency

represents a view so different from mine (though quite equally
legitimate), that it would hardly have served my present purpose.

to their associated ideas alone — it appeals also to that mysterious power by which mere arrangements of sound can convey an emotion which no one could have predicted beforehand, and which no known laws can explain.

It is true that the limits of melody within which poetry works are very narrow. Between an exquisite and a worthless line there is no difference of sound in any way noticeable to an unintelligent ear. For the mere volume of sound — the actual sonority of the passage — is a quite subordinate element in the effect, which is produced mainly by relations and sequences of vowels and consonants, too varying and delicate to be reproducible by rule, although far more widely similar, among European languages at least, than is commonly perceived.[1] But this limitation of the means employed, which may itself be an added source of pleasure from the sense which it may give of difficulty overcome, is by no means without analogies in other forms of art. The poet thrills us with delight by a collocation of consonants, much as the etcher suggests infinity by a scratch of the needle.

---

[1] An interesting confirmation of this statement may be obtained by reading some passage of Latin poetry first according to the English and then according to the Italian or the revived Latin pronunciation. The effects observed in the first case are not altered—are merely enriched—by the transference of the vowel sounds to another scale. But this natural music of language (if we may so term it) is too complex a subject to be more than touched on here.

And, indeed, in poetry of the first order, almost every word (to use a mathematical metaphor) is raised to a higher power. It continues to be an articulate sound and a logical step in the argument; but it becomes also a musical sound and a centre of emotional force. It becomes a musical sound;— that is to say, its consonants and vowels are arranged to bear a relation to the consonants and vowels near it, — a relation of which accent, quantity, rhyme, assonance, and alliteration are specialised forms, but which may be of a character more subtle than any of these. And it becomes a centre of emotional force; that is to say, the complex associations which it evokes modify the associations evoked by other words in the same passage in a way quite distinct from grammatical or logical connection. The poet, therefore, must avoid two opposite dangers. If he thinks too exclusively of the music and the colouring of his verse — of the imaginative means of suggesting thought and feeling — what he writes will lack reality and sense. But if he cares only to communicate definite thought and feeling according to the ordinary laws of eloquent speech, his verse is likely to be deficient in magical and suggestive power.

And what is meant by the vague praise so often bestowed on Virgil's unequalled style is practically this, that he has been, perhaps, more successful than any other poet in fusing together the expressed and the suggested emotion; that he has discovered the hidden music which can give to every shade of feeling its distinction, its permanence, and its charm; that his thoughts seem to come to us on the wings of melodies prepared for them from the foundation of the world. But in treating of so airy and abstract a matter it is well to have frequent recourse to concrete illustration. Before we attempt further description of Virgil's style, or his habitual mood of mind, let us clear our conceptions by a careful examination of some few passages from his poems. As we turn the leaves of the book we find it hard to know on what passages it were best to dwell. What varied memories are stirred by one line after another as we read! What associations of all dates, from Virgil's own lifetime down to the political debates of to-day! On this line[1] the poet's own voice faltered as he read. At this[2] Augustus and Octavia melted into passionate weeping. Here is the verse[3] which Augustine quotes as typical in its majestic rhythm of all the pathos and the glory of pagan art, from which the Christian was bound to flee. This is the couplet[4] which Fénelon could never read without admiring tears. This line Filippo Strozzi scrawled on his prison-wall, when he slew himself to avoid worse ill.[5] These are the words[6] which, like a trumpet-call,

---

[1] Hoc solum nomen quoniam de conjuge restat.   A. iv. 324.
[2] Tu Marcellus eris, etc.   A. vi. 883.
[3] Infelix simulacrum atque ipsius umbra Creusae.   A. ii. 772.
[4] Aude, hospes, contemnere opes, et te quoque dignum
    Finge deo, rebusque veni non asper egenis.   A. viii. 364.
[5] Exoriare aliquis nostris ex ossibus ultor.   A. iv. 625.
[6] Heu! fuge crudelis terras, fuge litus avarum.   A. iii. 44.

roused Savonarola to seek the things that are above.
And this line [1] Dante heard on the lips of the
Church Triumphant, at the opening of the Paradise
of God.   Here, too, are the long roll of prophecies,
sought tremblingly in the monk's secret cell, or echoing in the ears of emperors [2] from Apollo's shrine,
which have answered the appeal made by so many
an eager heart to the Virgilian Lots—that strange
invocation which has been addressed, I believe, to
Homer, Virgil, and the Bible alone; the offspring
of men's passionate desire to bring to bear on their
own lives the wisdom and the beauty which they
revered in the past, to make their prophets in such
wise as they might—

> " Speak from those lips of immemorial speech,
>   If but one word for each."

Such references might be multiplied indefinitely.
But there is not at any rate need to prove the
estimation in which Virgil has been held in the
past.   The force of that tradition would only be
weakened by specification.   " The chastest poet,"
in Bacon's words, " and royalest, Virgilius Maro,
that to the memory of man is known," has lacked
in no age until our own the concordant testimony
of the civilised world.   No poet has lain so close
to so many hearts ; no words so often as his have

---

[1] Manibus date lilia plenis. A. vi. 884.

[2] Claudius, Hadrian, Severus, etc., "in templo Apollinis
Cumani."

sprung to men's lips in moments of excitement and
self-revelation, from the one fierce line retained and
chanted by the untameable boy who was to be
Emperor of Rome,[1] to the impassioned prophecy of
the great English statesman[2] as he pleaded till morning's light for the freedom of a continent of slaves.

And those who have followed by more secret
ways the influence which these utterances have
exercised on mankind know well, perhaps themselves have shared, the mass of emotion which has
slowly gathered round certain lines of Virgil's as it
has round certain texts of the Bible, till they come
to us charged with more than an individual passion
and with a meaning wider than their own—with
the cry of the despair of all generations,[3] with the
yearning of all loves unappeased,[4] with the anguish
of all partings,[5] "beneath the pressure of separate
eternities."

Perhaps there will be no better way of forming
an intimate conception of the poet's own nature
than by analysing his treatment of two or three of

---

[1] Clodius Albinus.   Arma amens capio ; nec sat rationis in
armis. A. ii. 314.

[2] Pitt. G. i. 250.
    Nosque ubi primus equis Oriens adflavit anhelis,
    Illic sera rubens accendit lumina Vesper.

[3] Quo res summa loco, Panthu ? quam prendimus arcem ? A.
ii. 322.

[4] Illum absens absentem auditque videtque. A. iv. 83.

[5] Quem fugis ? extremum fato, quod te adloquor, hoc est. A.
vi. 466.

his principal characters, and especially of his hero, so often considered as forming the weakest element in his poem. Æneas, no doubt, looks at once tame and rigid beside the eager and spontaneous warriors of the Homeric epoch, and, so far as the Æneid is a poem of action and adventure, he is not a stirring or an appropriate hero. But we must not forget that there was a special difficulty in making his character at once consistent and attractive. He is a man who has survived his strongest passion, his deepest sorrow; who has seen his "Ilium settle into flame," and from "Creusa's melancholy shade," and the great ghost of Hector fallen in vain, has heard the words which sum the last disaster and close the tale of Troy. It is no fault of his that he is left alive; and the poem opens with the cry of his regret that he too has not been able to fall dead upon the Trojan plain, "where Hector lies, and huge Sarpedon, and Simois rolls so many warriors' corses to the sea." But it is not always at a man's crowning moment that his destiny and his duty close; and for those who fain had perished with what they held most dear, fate may reserve a more tedious trial, and the sad triumphs of a life whose sun has set. It is to this note that all the adventures of Æneas respond. We find him when he lands at Carthage at once absorbed in the pictures which show the story of Priam and of his city's fall—

" What realm of earth, he answered, doth not know,
　O friend, our sad pre-eminence of woe ?
　Tears waken tears, and honour honour brings,
　And mortal hearts are moved by mortal things." [1]

Then he himself tells that tale, with an intensity of
pathos too well known to need further allusion.
And when his story brings him to calmer scenes—
to his meeting with " Hector's Andromache " on the
Chaonian shore — those who have loved and lost
will recognise in their colloquy the touches that
paint the fond illusion of the heart which clings,
with a half smile at its own sad persistency, to the
very name and semblance of the places by love
made dear,[2] which seeks in the eyes or movements
of surviving kindred some glance or gesture of the
dead.[3]   Take one more instance only—the meeting
of Æneas with Deiphobus in the underworld—and
note how the same cry breaks from him [4] as that
with which he greeted the vision of Hector,[5] — a
cry of reverence heightened by compassion — that

---

[1] Quis jam locus, inquit, Achate,
Quae regio in terris nostri non plena laboris ?
En Priamus ! sunt hic etiam sua praemia laudi ;
Sunt lacrimae rerum, et mentem mortalia tangunt. A. i. 459.

[2] Procedo, et parvam Troiam simulataque magnis
Pergama et arentem Xanthi cognomine rivum
Adgnosco, Scaeaeque amplector limina portae.   A. iii. 349.

[3] Cape dona extrema tuorum
O mihi sola mei super Astyanactis imago !
Sic oculos, sic ille manus, sic ora ferebat ;
Et nunc aequali tecum pubesceret aevo.   A. iii. 488.

[4] A. vi. 502.   [5] A. ii. 285.

mingling of emotions which makes the utmost
ardour of worship and of love—a cry of indignation
such as rends the generous heart at the sight of an
exalted spirit on which vileness and treachery have
been allowed to work their will. How delicately
does the "anima cortese Mantovana" stand revealed
in the lofty reverence with which Æneas addresses
the maimed Deiphobus,[1] even while he "hardly
knows him, as he trembles and strives to hide his
ghastly wounds!" How strangely sweet the cadence
in which the living friend laments that he could
not see that other, as he lay in death,[2] could only
invoke his spirit with a threefold salutation, and
rear an empty tomb! In such sad converse Æneas
loses the brief time granted for his visit to the
underworld, till the Sibyl warns him that it is
being spent in vain—

> "The night is going, Trojan; shall it go
> Lost in an aimless memory of woe?"[3]

But he does not part from his murdered friend till
he has given the assurance that all that could be
done has been done; that he has paid the utter-
most honour and satisfied the unforgetful shade.

Yet once more; perhaps the deepest note of all
is struck when the old love is encountered by a
new, and yet both that memory and that fresh joy

---

[1] Deiphobe armipotens, genus alto a sanguine Teucri. A. vi. 500.
[2] A. vi. 507.
[3] Nox ruit, Aenea, nos flendo ducimus horas. A. vi. 539.

must give place to an over-ruling call.   When Dido
implores Æneas to remain in Carthage, after the messenger of Jove has bidden him depart, he answers in
words whose solemn movement reveals a long-un-
uttered pain, and shows that neither in Carthage,
nor yet in Italy, can his heart expect a home [1]—

> " Me had the fates allowed my woes to still,—
> Take my sad life, and shape it at my will,—
> First had I sought my buried home and joy,
> Loves unforgotten, and the last of Troy ;—
> Ay, Priam's palace had re-risen then,
> A ghost of Ilium for heart-broken men."

It is thus that the solemn appeal evokes the
unlooked-for avowal; once and for all he makes it
known that the memory which to others is growing
dim and half-forgotten in the past, is to him ever
present and ever guiding, and always and unalterably
dear.

No doubt it is probable that Virgil would have
been ill able to describe a more buoyant and adventurous hero.   No doubt it is true that such a
nature as that of Æneas is ill fitted to fill the leading *rôle* in a poem of action.   But granting that we
have him here in the wrong place, and should have
preferred a character whom the poet could not draw,
we yet surely cannot say, when we remember Æneas'
story, that the picture given of him is meaningless
or untrue; we cannot call it unnatural that we

---

[1] A. iv. 340.

should find in all his conduct something predetermined, hieratic, austere; we cannot wonder if the only occasion on which he rises to passionate excitement is where he implores the Sibyl for pity's sake to bring him to the sight and presence of the soul he holds so dear;[1] or if, when from that soul in Paradise he has learnt the secrets of the dead, his temper thenceforth is rather that of the Christian saint than of the Pagan warrior, and he becomes the type of those mediæval heroes, those Galahads and Percivals, whose fiercest exploits are performed with a certain remoteness of spirit — who look beyond blood and victory to a concourse of unseen spectators and a sanction that is not of men.

It is, however, on another character that the personal interest of the Æneid has been generally felt to turn. The story of Dido has been said to mark the dawn of romance. It is no doubt the case, though how far this is accidental it is hard to say, that the ancients have dealt oftener with the tragedies resulting from the passion of love, than with the delineation of that passion itself. Sappho, in her early world, had written, as it were, the epigraph over love's temple-door in letters of fire. Catullus had caught the laughing glory of Septimius and Acme—of amorous girl and boy; Lucretius had painted, with all the mastering force of Rome, the pangs of passion baffled by its own intensity and

[1] A. vi. 117

festering unsated in a heart at war.   But once only, perhaps, do we find the joy of love's appearing, the desolation of his flight, sung of before Virgil's days with a majesty and a pathos like his own.   No one who has read has forgotten how " once to Ilion's towers there seemed to come the spirit of a windless calm—a gentle darling of wealth, soft dart of answering eyes, love's soul-subduing flower."   Few have heard unmoved of the " semblances of mournful dreams " which brought to that deserted husband " an empty joy; for all in vain, when his delight he seemed to see, forth gliding from his arms the vision vanished far, on swift wings following the ways of sleep."   In Æschylus, as in Virgil, the story derives its pathos from the severing of happy loves.   In Æschylus they are separated by the woman's misdoing; in Virgil by a higher obligation which the man is bidden to fulfil, yet an obligation which the woman bitterly denies, and which we are ourselves half unwilling to allow.   Neither of these plots is quite satisfactory.   For in the atmosphere of noble · poetry we cannot readily endure that love should either be marred by sin or unreconciled with duty; and no cause of lovers' separation is in harmony with our highest mood, unless it be the touch of death, whose power is but a momentary thing, or so high a call of honour as can give to the parting death's promise and not only his pain.

The power with which Dido is drawn is unques-

tionable. Her transitions of feeling, her ardent
soliloquies, reveal a dramatic force in Virgil of a very
unexpected kind—an insight into the female heart
which is seldom gained by the exercise of imagination alone. But when we compare the Fourth
Æneid with later poems on the same lofty level—
with the *Vita Nuova*, for instance, or with *Laodamia*
—we feel how far our whole conception of woman-
hood has advanced since Virgil's day under the
influence of Christianity, chivalry, civilisation. A
nature like Dido's will now repel as much as it
attracts us. For we have learnt that a woman may
be childlike as well as impassioned, and soft as well
as strong; that she may glow with all love's fire
and yet be delicately obedient to the lightest whisper
of honour. The most characteristic factor in Dido's
story is of a more external kind. It is the contrast
between the queen's stately majesty and the subduing power of love which is most effectively used
to intensify the dramatic situation. And the picture
suggests a few reflections as to the way in which the
wealth and magnificence of Roman society affected
the poets of the age.

It happens that three great Latin poets, in strik-
ingly similar passages,[1] have drawn the contrast
between a simple and a splendid life. Horace, here,
as elsewhere, shows himself the ideal poet of society;
more cultivated, sensitive, affectionate than the men

[1] Lucr. ii. 24. Virg. G. ii. 468. Hor. Carm. iii. 1, 41.

and women among whom he moves, yet not so far above them or aloof from them but that he can delight, even more keenly than they, in their luxury and splendour — can enjoy it without envy, as he can dispense with it without regret. Lucretius is the aristocrat with a mission; to him the lamp-bearing images, and the blaze of midnight banquets, and the harp that echoes beneath the ceiling's fretted gold—all these are but a vain and bitter jest which cannot drive superstition from the soul, nor kill those fears of death which "mingle unabashed amongst kings and kesars," awed not at all by golden glitter or by purple sheen. Virgil is the rustic of genius, well educated, of delicately refined nature, wholly free from base admirations or desires, but "reared amid the woods and copses," and retaining to the last some touch of shyness in the presence of this world's grandeur; ever eager to escape from the palace-halls into his realm of solitude and song. The well-known passage in the Georgics depicts, as we may well imagine, in its vein of dignified irony, his own sensations when he mixed with the society which so eagerly sought him at Rome. We have his embarrassment at the crowd of visitors coming and going as he calls on Pollio or Mæcenas at the fashionable hour of 7 A.M.; his ennui as he ac-companies over the house a party of virtuosi, open-mouthed at the æsthetic furniture; and even his disgust at the uncomfortable magnificence of his

bedchamber, and at the scented oil which is served
to him with his salad at dinner.[1]   And what a
soaring change when from the stately metrical roll
which reflects the pomp and luxury of the imperial
city, he mounts without an effort into that airy rush
which blends together all "the glory of the divine
country," its caverns, and its living lakes, and haunts
of wild things in the glade, its "life that never dis-
appoints," its life-long affections, and its faith in
God ![2]

Yet Virgil's familiarity with the statelier life of
Rome was not unfruitful.   It has given to him in his
Æneid an added touch of dignity, as of one who has
seen face to face such greatness as earth can offer,
and paints without misgiving the commerce of
potentates and kings.   And thus it is that he has
filled every scene of Dido's story with a sense of
royal scope and unchartered power ; as of an existence where all honours are secure already, and all
else that is wished for won, only the heart demands
an inner sanctuary, and life's magnificence still lacks
its crowning joy.   First we have the banquet, when
love is as yet unacknowledged and unknown, but
the "signs of his coming and sounds of his feet"

[1] Si non ingentem foribus domus alta superbis
Mane salutantum totis vomit aedibus undam,
Nec varios inhiant pulchra testudine postis,
Inlusasque auro vestes, Ephyreiaque aera,
Alba neque Assyrio fucatur lana veneno,
Nec casia liquidi corrumpitur usus olivi.   G. ii. 461.
[2] G. ii. 473.

have begun to raise all things to an intenser glow;
when the singer's song rises more glorious, and all
voices ring more full and free,[1] and ancestral ceremonies are kindled into life by the ungovernable
gladness of the soul.[2]   Then comes the secluded
colloquy between queen and princess,[3] as they discuss the guest who made the night so strange and
new; and then the rush of Dido's gathering passion
among the majestic symbols of her sway.[4]

> "With him the queen the long ways wanders down,
> And shows him Sidon's wealth and Carthage town,
> And oft would speak, but as the words begin
> Fails her breath caught by mastering Love within;—
> Once more in feast must she the night employ,
> Must hear once more her Trojan tell of Troy,
> Hang on his kingly voice, and shuddering see
> The imagined scenes where every scene is he.
> Then guests are gone and night and morn are met,
> Far off in heaven the solemn stars have set,—
> Thro' the empty halls alone she mourns again,
> Lies on the couch where hath her hero lain,
> Sees in the dark his kingly face, and hears
> His voice imagined in her amorous ears."

And through all the scenes that follow, the same
royal accent runs till the last words that lift our
imagination from the tumultuous grief around the
dying Dido, to the scarce more terrible tragedy of
a great nation's fall.[5]

---

[1] A. i. 725.   [2] A. i. 738.   [3] A. iv. 10.
[4] A. iv. 74.   [5] A. iv. 669.

" Not else than thus, when foes have forced a way,
On Tyre or Carthage falls the fatal day ;—
'Mid such wild woe crash down in roaring fire
Temples and towers of Carthage or of Tyre."

And assuredly the " Deeds of the Roman People,"[1]
the title which many men gave to the Æneid when
it first appeared, would not have been complete
without some such chapter as this.   The prophecy
of Anchises, the shield of Vulcan, record for us the
imperial city's early virtue, her world-wide sway ;
but it is in this tale of Carthage that the poet has
written in a burning parable the passion and the
pomp of Rome.

And yet in spite of all the force and splendour
with which Dido is described, we feel instinctively
that she is not drawn by a lover's hand.   We have
in her no indication of the poet's own ideal and
inward dream.   If that is to be sought at all, it
must be sought elsewhere.   And, perhaps, if the
fancy be permitted, we may imagine that we discern
it best in the strange and yearning beauty of the
passages which speak of the glorious girlhood of
Camilla, the maid unwon ; Camilla, whose death a
nymph avenges, and whose tale Diana tells; Camilla,
whose name leapt first of all to Virgil's lips as he
spoke to Dante of their Italy in the underworld.[2]
Surely there is something more than a mere poetic fervour in the lines which describe the love which lit on

---

[1] "Gesta populi Romani."   [2] Inf. i. 107.

the girl while yet a child, and followed her till her glorious hour;[1] the silent reverence which watched the footsteps of the maiden "whom so many mothers for their sons desired in vain;"[2] the breath caught with a wistful wonder, the long and lingering gaze,[3] the thrill of admiration which stirs the heart with the very concord of joy and pain. Where has he more subtly mingled majesty with sweetness than in the lines which paint her happy nurture among the woodlands where her father was a banished king? her wild and supple strength enhanced by the contrasting thought of the "flowing gown and golden circlet,"[4] which might have weighted the free limbs with royal purple or wound among the tresses that were hooded with the tiger's spoil.

Thus much, at least, we may say, that while in poetry the higher and truer forms of love, as distinguished both from friendship and from passion, appear first in the Middle Ages, and in Dante above all, yet passages like these reveal to us the early stirring of conceptions which were hereafter to be so dominant and so sublime—the dawning instinct of

[1] A. xi. 537.   [2] A. xi. 581.

[3] Illam omnis tectis agrisque effusa inventus
    Turbaque miratur matrum et prospectat euntem,
    Attonitis inhians animis, ut regius ostro
    Velet honos levis humeros, ut fibula crinem
    Auro internectat, Lyciam ut gerat ipsa pharetram
    Et pastoralem praefixa cuspide myrtum.—A. vii. 812.

[4] Pro crinali auro, pro longae tegmine pallae
    Tigridis exuviae per dorsum a vertice pendent, etc.—A. xi. 576.

a worship which should be purer and more pervading than any personal desire—of a reverence which should have power for a season to keep Love himself at bay, and to which a girl's gladness and beauty should become a part " of something far more deeply interfused," and touch the spirit with the same sense of yearning glory which descends on us from the heaven of stars.

To dwell thus on some of the passages in Virgil whose full meaning escapes a hasty perusal, may help us to realise one of his characteristic charms —his power of concentrating the strangeness and fervour of the romantic spirit within the severe and dignified limits of classical art. To this power in great measure we must ascribe his unique position as the only unbroken link between the ancient and the modern world. In literary style and treatment, just as in religious dogma and tendency, there has been something in him which has appealed in turn to ages the most discrepant and the most remote. He has been cited in different centuries as an authority on the worship of river-nymphs and on the incarnation of Christ. And similarly the poems which were accepted as soon as published as the standard of Latin classicality, became afterwards the direct or indirect original of half the Renaissance epics of adventure and love.

We feel, however, that considerations like these leave us still far from any actual realisation of the means by which the poet managed to produce this singular complex of impressions. In dealing with poetry, as with the kindred arts, criticism almost necessarily ceases to be fruitful or definite at the very point where the interest of the problems becomes the greatest. We must be content with such narrower inquiries as may give us at least a clearer conception of the nature and difficulties of the achievement at which the artist has aimed. We may, for instance, discuss the capabilities of the particular language in which a poet writes, just as we may discuss the kind of effects producible on violin or pianoforte, in water-colour or oil. And any estimate of the Latin, as a literary language, implies at once a comparison with the speech of that people from whose admirable productions Latin literature was avowedly derived.

No words that men can any more set side by side can ever affect the mind again like some of the great passages of Homer. For in them it seems as if all that makes life precious were in the act of being created at once and together—language itself, and the first emotions, and the inconceivable charm of song. When we hear one single sentence of Anticleia's answer,[1] as she begins—

οὔτ᾽ ἔμεγ᾽ ἐν μεγαροῖσιν ἐΰσκοπος ἰοχέαιρα—

what words can express the sense which we receive

[1] Od. xi. 198.

of an effortless and absolute sublimity, the feeling
of morning freshness and elemental power, the
delight which is to all other intellectual delights
what youth is to all other joys? And what a
language! which has written, as it were, of itself
those last two words for the poet, which offers them
as the fruit of its inmost structure and the bloom
of its early day! Beside speech like this Virgil's
seems elaborate, and Dante's crabbed, and Shake-
speare's barbarous. There never has been, there
never will be, a language like the dead Greek. For
Greek had all the merits of other tongues without
their accompanying defects. It had the monu-
mental weight and brevity of the Latin without its
rigid unmanageability; the copiousness and flexi-
bility of the German without its heavy commonness
and guttural superfluity; the pellucidity of the
French without its jejuneness; the force and reality
of the English without its structureless comminu-
tion. But it was an instrument beyond the control
of any but its creators. When the great days of
Greece were past, it was the language which made
speeches and wrote books, and not the men. Its
French brilliancy taught Isocrates to polish platitude
into epigram; its German profundity enabled Lyco-
phron to pass off nonsense as oracles; its Italian
flow encouraged Apollonius Rhodius to shroud in
long-drawn sweetness the langour of his inventive
soul. There was nothing except the language left.

Like the golden brocade in a queen's sepulchre, its imperishable splendour was stretched stiffly across the skeleton of a life and thought which inhabited there no more.

The history of the Latin tongue was widely different. We do not meet it full-grown at the dawn of history; we see it take shape and strength beneath our eyes. We can watch, as it were, each stage in the forging of the thunderbolt; from the day when Ennius, Nævius, Pacuvius inweave their "three shafts of twisted storm,"[1] till Lucretius adds "the sound and terror," and Catullus "the west wind and the fire." It grows with the growth of the Roman people; it wins its words at the sword's point; and the "conquered nations in long array" pay tribute of their thought and speech as surely as of their blood and gold.

In the region of poetry this union of strenuous effort with eager receptivity is conspicuously seen. The barbarous Saturnian lines, hovering between an accentual and a quantitative system, which were the only indigenous poetical product of Latium, rudely indicated the natural tendency of the Latin tongue towards a trochaic rhythm. Contact with Greece introduced Greek metres, and gradually established a definite quantitative system. Quantity and accent are equally congenial to the Latin lan-

---

[1] Tris imbris torti radios, tris nubis aquosae
Addiderant, rutili tris ignis et alitis Austri.   A. viii. 429.

guage, and the trochaic and iambic metres of Greece bore transplantation with little injury. The adaptations of these rhythms by early Roman authors, however uncouth, are at least quite easy and unconstrained; and so soon as the prestige of the Augustan era had passed away, we find both Pagans and Christians expressing in accentual iambic, and especially in accentual trochaic metres, the thoughts and feelings of the new age. Adam of S. Victor is metrically nearer to Livius Andronicus than to Virgil or Ovid; and the Litany of the Arval Brethren finds its true succession, not in the Secular Ode of Horace, but in the *Dies Iræ* or the *Veni Creator*.

For Latin poetry suffered a violent breach of continuity in the introduction from Greece of the hexameter and the elegiac couplet. The quantitative hexameter is in Latin a difficult and unnatural metre. Its prosodial structure excludes a very large proportion of Latin words from being employed at all. It narrowly limits the possible grammatical constructions, the modes of emphasis, the usages of curtailment, the forms of narration. On the other hand, when successfully managed its advantages are great. All the strength and pregnancy of Latin expression are brought out by the stately march of a metre perhaps the most compact and majestic which has ever been invented. The words take their place like the organs in a living structure—

close packed but delicately adjusted and mutually supporting. And the very sense of difficulty overcome gives an additional charm to the sonorous beauty of the dactylic movement, its self-retarding pauses, its onward and overwhelming flow.

To the Greek the most elaborate poetical effects were as easy as the simplest. In his poetic, as in his glyptic art, he found all materials ready to his hand; he had but to choose between the marble and the sardonyx, between the ivory and the gold. The Roman hewed his conceptions out of the granite rock; oftenest its craggy forms were rudely piled together, yet dignified and strong; but there were hands which could give it finish too, which could commit to the centuries a work splendid as well as imperishable, polished into the basalt's shimmer and fervent with the porphyry's glow.

It must not, however, be supposed that even the Æneid has wholly overcome the difficulties inseparable from the Latin poetry of the classical age, that it is entirely free either from the frigidities of an imitation or from the constraints of a *tour de force*. In the first place, Virgil has not escaped the injury which has been done to subsequent poets by the example of the length and the subject-matter of Homer. An artificial dignity has been attached to poems in twelve or twenty-four books, and authors have been incited to tell needlessly long stories in order to take rank as epic poets. And because

Homer is full of tales of personal combat—in his day an exciting and all-important thing — later poets have thought it necessary to introduce a large element of this kind of description, which, so soon as it loses reality, becomes not only frigid but disgusting. It is as if the first novel had been written by a schoolboy of genius, and all succeeding novelists had felt bound to construct their plots mainly of matches at football. It is the later books of the Æneid that are most marred by this mistake. In the earlier books there are, no doubt, some ill-judged adaptations of Homeric incident,[1] some laboured reproductions of Homeric formulæ, but for the most part the events are really noble and pathetic,—are such as possess permanent interest for civilised men. The three last books, on the other hand, which have come down to us in a crude and unpruned condition, contain large tracts immediately imitated from Homer, and almost devoid of independent value.[2]

Besides these defects in matter, the latter part of the poem illustrates the metrical dangers to which Latin hexameters succumbed almost as soon as Virgil was gone. The types on which they could be composed were limited in number and were becoming exhausted. Many of the lines in

---

[1] See especially A. v. 263-5.

[2] The following passages might perhaps be omitted *en bloc* with little injury to Virgil's reputation :—A. x. 276-762 ; xi. 597-648, 868-908 ; xii. 266-311, 529-592.

the later books are modelled upon lines in the
earlier ones. Many passages show that peculiar
form of bald artificiality into which this difficult
metre so readily sinks; nay, some of the *tibicines*,
or stop-gaps, suggest a grotesque resemblance to the
well-known style of the fourth-form boy.[1] Other
more ambitious passages give the painful impression
of just missing the effect at which they aim.[2]

We should, however, be much mistaken if we
inferred that this accidental want of finish—due to
the poet's premature death—indicated any decline
of power. On the contrary, nothing, perhaps, in
Latin versification is more interesting than the
traces of a later manner in process of formation,
which are to be found in the concluding books of
the Æneid. The later manner of a painter or poet
generally differs from his earlier manner in much
the same way. We observe in him a certain im-
patience of the rules which have guided him to
excellence, a certain desire to use materials more
freely, to obtain bolder and newer effects. A
tendency of this kind may be discerned in the
versification of the later books, especially of the
twelfth book, of the Æneid. The innovations are
individually hardly perceptible, but taken together
they alter the character of the hexameter line in a
way more easily felt than described. Among the
more definite changes we may note that there are

[1] *e.g.* A. x. 526-9, 584-5.   [2] *e.g.* A. x. 468-471, 557-560.

more full stops in the middle of lines, there are more elisions, there is a larger proportion of short words, there are more words repeated, more assonances, and a freer use of the emphasis gained by the recurrence of verbs in the same or cognate tenses.   Where passages thus characterised have come down to us still in the making, the effect is forced and fragmentary.[1]   Where they succeed they combine, as it seems to me, in a novel manner the rushing freedom of the old trochaics with the majesty which is the distinguishing feature of Virgil's style.[2]   Art has concealed its art, and the poet's last words suggest to us possibilities in the Latin tongue which no successor has been able to realise.

It is difficult to dwell long on such technical points as these without appearing arbitrary or pedantic.   The important thing is to understand how deliberate, forceful, weighty, Virgil's diction is ; what a mass of thought and feeling was needed to give to the elaborate structure of the Latin hexameter any convincing power ; how markedly all those indications by which we instinctively judge the truth or the insincerity of an author's emotion are intensified by a form of composition in which " the style," not only of every paragraph but of every clause, is

---

[1] *e.g.* A. x. 597-600.

[2] *e.g.* A. xii. 48, 72, 179, 429, 615-6, 632-649, 676-680, 889-893, 903-4.

necessarily and indeed "the man." And when we
have learned by long familiarity to read between the
lines, to apportion the emphasis, to reproduce, it may
be, in imagination some shadow of that " marvellous
witchery "[1] with which, as tradition tells us, Virgil's
own reading of his poems brought out their beauty,
we shall be surprised at the amount of self-revelation
discernible beneath the calm of his impersonal song.
And here again we shall receive the same impression
which remained with us from the examination of the
hero who is thought to be in some measure the unconscious portrait of the poet himself—we shall
wonder most of all at the abiding sadness of his soul.

We might have thought to find him like the
steersman Palinurus, in the scene from which our
great English painter has taken the cadence which
is to tell of an infinite repose,[2] communing untroubled
with some heaven-descended dream, and keeping
through the night's tranquillity his eyes still fixed
upon the stars. How is it that he appears to us so
often, like the same Palinurus, plunged in a solitary
gulf of death, while the ship of human destinies drifts
away unguided—*trostlos auf weitem Meer?* How
knew he that gathering horror of midnight which
presages some unspeakable ruin and the end of all?[3]
Why was it left for him, above all men, to tell of the
anguish of irredeemable bereavement, and Eurydice's

---

[1] "Lenociniis miris."
[2] Turner's Datur Hora Quieti. A. v. 844.　　[3] A. iv. 460-4.

appealing hands as she vanished backwards into the
night ?[1]   What taught him the passion of those lines
whose marvellous versification seems to beat with
the very pulses of the heart,[2] where the one soul calls
upon the other in the many-peopled fields of death,
and asks of all that company, " not less nor more, but
even that word alone " ?   What is it that has given
such a mystical intensity to every glimpse which he
opens of the eternity of the impassioned soul? —
where sometimes the wild pathetic rhythm alone
suggests an undefinable regret,[3] or a single epithet
will renew a world of mourning, and disclose a sorrow unassuageable in Paradise itself.[4]   Or, for one
moment, Sychaeus' generous shade, appealed to in
such varying accents as the storms of passion rose
or fell, deemed sometimes forgetful and distant and
unregarding in the grave, is seen at last in very
presence and faithful to the vows of earth, filled
with a love which has forgiven inconstancy as it has
outlasted death.[5]

These short and pregnant passages will appeal to
different minds with very different power.   There
are some whose emotion demands a fuller expression
than this, a more copious and ready flow—who choose
rather, like Shelley, to pour the whole free nature
into a sudden and untrammelled lay.   But there are
others who have learnt to recognise the last height

---

[1] G. iv. 498.   [2] A. vi. 670.
[3] A. vi. 447.   [4] A. vi. 480.   [5] A. vi. 474.

of heroism, the last depth of tenderness, rather in a
word than in a protest, and rather in a look than in a
word; to whom all strong feeling comes as a purging
fire, a disengagement from the labyrinth of things;
whose passion takes a more concentrated dignity as
it turns inwards and to the deep of the heart. And
such men will recognise in Virgil a precursor, a master,
and a friend; they will call him the *Magnanimo*, the
Verace Duca; they will enrol themselves with eager
loyalty among the spiritual progeny of a spirit so
melancholy, august, and alone.

And some, too, there will always be to whom
some touch of poetic gift has revealed the delight of
self-expression, while yet their infertile instinct of
melody has failed them at their need, and their
scanty utterance has rather mocked than assuaged for
them the incommunicable passion of the soul. Such
men will be apt to think that not only would an
added sanctity have been given to all sacred sorrow,
an added glory to all unselfish joy, but that this
earth's less ennobling emotions as well—the sting
of unjust suspicions,[1] and the proud resentment of
stealthy injuries,[2] and the bewilderment of life's unguided way[3]—even these would have been trans-
muted into spiritual strength if they could in such
manner have shaped themselves into song; as the
noise of bear, and wolf, and angered lion came to the
Trojans with a majesty that had no touch of fear or

[1] A. i. 529.   [2] A. vi. 502.   [3] A. xii. 917.

pain, as they heard them across the midnight waters, mixed with the music of Circe's echoing isle.[1]

How was it, then, with the poet himself, to whom it was given to "sweep in ever-highering eagle-circles up" till his words became the very term and limit of human utterance in song? *Quin Decios Drusosque procul ;*—when he was summing up in those lines like bars of gold the hero-roll of the Eternal City, conferring with every word an immortality, and, like his own Æneas, bearing on his shoulders the fortune and the fame of Rome, did he feel in that great hour that he had done all that man can do? All that we know is, that he spoke of his attempt to write the Æneid as "an act almost of insanity," and that on his deathbed he urgently begged his friends to burn the unfinished poem.

> " O dignitosa coscienza e netta,
>   Come t'è picciol fallo amaro morso ! "

Yet we feel that Virgil's character would not have stood out complete to us without the record of that last desire. It was the culminating expression of a lifelong temper—of that yearning after perfection which can never rest satisfied with the things of earth—which carries always with it, as Plato would say, the haunting reminiscence of that perfect beauty on which the soul has looked aforetime in the true, which is the ideal world. And the very stillness

[1] A. vii. 10.

and dignity of Virgil's outward existence help to
make him to us an unmixed example of this mood
of mind. There is no trace in him of egoistic passion,
of tumult, of vanity, or of any jealous or eager love ;
all his emotions seem to have fused or melted into
that *Welt-Schmerz*—that impersonal and indefinable
melancholy, the sound of which since his day has
grown so familiar in our ears, which invades the
sanest and the strongest spirits, and seems to yield
to nothing except such a love, or such a faith, as can
give or promise heaven. The so-called " modern air "
in Virgil's poems is in great measure the result of
the constantly-felt pressure of this obscure home-
sickness—this infinite desire ; finding vent sometimes
in such appeals as forestall the sighs of Christian
saints in the passion of high hopes half withdrawn,
when the Divinity is shrouded and afar[1]—oftener
perceptible only in that accent of brooding sorrow
which mourns over the fate of men, and breathes a
pathetic murmur into Nature's peace,[2] and touches
with a mysterious forlornness the felicity of the
underworld.[3]

It is the same mood which " intenerisce il cuore "
in Dante's song, which looks from the unsatisfied
eyes of Michael Angelo and of Tintoret,—a mood
commoner, indeed, among the nations of the North,

---

[1] *e.g.* G. iv. 324-5. A. i. 407.

[2] Te nemus Anguitiae, vitrea te Fucinus unda,
Te liquidi flevere lacus. A. vii. 760.

[3] Solemque suum, sua sidera nôrunt. A. vi. 641.

but felt at times by Italians who have had the power to see that all the glory round them does but add a more mysterious awfulness to the insoluble riddle of the world.

Nor is any region of Italy a fitter temple for such thoughts than the Bay of Naples, which virtually was Virgil's home.   For it was not Mantua, but " sweet Parthenope," which fostered his years of silent toil ; his wanderings were on that southern shore where the intense and azure scene seems to carry an unknown sadness in.the convergence of heaven and sea, and something of an unearthly expectancy in the still magnificence of its glow.   It was there that inwardly he bled and was comforted, inwardly he suffered and was strong; it was there that what others learn in tempest he learnt in calm, and became in ardent solitude the very voice and heart of Rome.

II.

The century which elapsed between the publication of the Fourth Eclogue and of the Epistle to the Romans witnessed an immense expansion of the human mind.   So far as we can attach definite dates to the gradual growth of world-wide conceptions, we may say that in this century arose the ideas of the civil and of the religious unity of all families of men. These ideas, at first apparently hostile to one another, and associated, the one with the military supremacy of Rome, the other with the spiritual supremacy of Jerusalem, gradually coalesced into the notion of a Holy Roman Empire, involving, as that notion does in the mind, for instance, of Dante, the concentration of both spiritual and temporal power in the Eternal City. Again the conceptions have widened; and we now imagine a brotherhood of mankind, a universal Church, without localised empire or a visible vice-gerent of heaven.

Throughout all the phases which these great generalisations have traversed, the authority of Virgil has been freely invoked. And when we turn from the personal to the public aspect of his poems, we are at once obliged to discuss in what sense he may be considered as the earliest and the official exponent of the world-wide Empire of Rome, the last and the closest precursor of the world-wide commonwealth of Christ. The unanimous acceptance of Virgil in his lifetime—while the Æneid was yet unwritten—as the unique poetical representative of the Roman State is a fact quite as surprising and significant as the ready acceptance of Augustus as its single ruler. It is not, indeed, strange that a few short but lovely pieces, such as the Eclogues, should have delighted literary circles and suggested to Mæcenas that this young poet's voice would be the fittest to preach the revival of antique simplicity and rural toil. The astonishing thing is the success of the Georgics, the fact that an agricultural poem not twice as long as

Comus should at once have procured for its author a
reputation to which the literary history of the world
affords no parallel.   Petrarch was crowned on the
Capitol amid the applause of the literati of Europe.
Voltaire was "smothered with roses" in the crowded
theatres of the Paris of his old age.   But the triumph
of Petrarch was the manifesto of a humanistic clique.
The triumph of Voltaire was the first thunderclap
of a political storm.   When, on the other hand, the
Romans rose to their feet in the theatre on the casual
quotation of some words of Virgil's on the stage—
when they saluted the poet as he entered the house
with the same marks of reverence which they paid
to Augustus Cæsar—it was plain that some cause
was at work which was not of a partisan, which was
not even of a purely literary character.   Perhaps it
was that the minds of men were agitated by the
belief that a new era was impending, that "the great
order of the ages was being born anew," and in the
majestic and catholic tranquillity of Virgil's song they
recognised instinctively the temper of an epoch no
longer of struggle but of supremacy, the first-fruits
of Imperial Rome.   We must at least attribute some
such view to the cultivated classes of the time.   That
the sublime poem of Lucretius should obtain only
a cold *succès d'estime*, while the Georgics, a more exquisite work, no doubt, but a work of so much smaller
range, should be hailed as raising its author to an
equality with Homer, is a disproportion too great to

be accounted for by a mere literary preference. It was a deep-seated recognition of the truly national character of Virgil's work, of his unique fitness to reflect completely all the greatness of the advancing time, which led even rival poets to predict so strenuously that the Æneid, of which no one had as yet seen a paragraph, would be co-eternal with the dominion of Rome. Stranger still it is to see how tragically the event surpassed the prophecy. "Light among the vanished ages," we may exclaim with no exaggeration, in Lord Tennyson's words—

> "Star that gildest yet this phantom shore !
> Golden branch amid the shadows, kings and realms that
> set to rise no more !"

When we look at the intellectual state of Rome in the fourth and fifth centuries, our complaint is not that Virgil is forgotten, but that nothing else is remembered ; that the last achievement of the " toga-wearing race " is to extemporise centos from the Æneid on any given theme ; that the last heads seen to rise above the flood of advancing barbarism should be those of grammarians calling themselves Menalcas and parsing *Tityre*, or calling themselves Virgilius and parsing *Arma virum*.

There is something, too, of Fate's solemn irony in the way in which, as the ancient world is re-discovered, the first words borne back to us by the muffled voice of ruin or catacomb are scattered

fragments of that poem which was the last on
Rome's living lips. There is something tragic in
finding Virgil's line, "So great a work it was to
found the race of Rome," cut in colossal characters
on the monstrous ruins of the baths of Titus;
Virgil's words, "Then all were silent," look strangely
in a half-finished scrawl from a wall of Pompeii's
hushed and solitary homes.[1] But the long tradition,
as has been already said, has not continued unbroken to our own day. There have of late been
many critics who have denied that the Æneid is
adequately representative of the Roman commonwealth, who have been struck with the unqualified
support, the absolute deification bestowed on
Augustus, and have urged that the laureate who
indulged in so gratuitous an adulation must be
styled a court, and not a national poet.

So far as Virgil's mere support of Augustus
goes, this objection, however natural to the lovers
of free government, will hardly stand the test of
historical inquiry. For Virgil had not to choose
between Augustus and the Republic, but between
Augustus and Antony. The Republic was gone for
ever; and not Hannibal himself, we may surely
say, was a more dangerous foe than Antony to the
Roman people. No battle which that people ever
fought was more thoroughly national, more decis-
ively important, than the battle of Actium. The

[1] CONTICVEREOM.

name of Actium, indeed, can never waken the glory
and the joy which spring to the heart at the name
of Salamis. Not "Leucate's promontory afire with
embattled armaments," not " Actian Apollo bending
from above his bow " can stir the soul like that one
trump,[1] that morning onset, that "small ill-har-
boured islet, oft-haunted of dance-loving Pan." [2]
But the essence of each battle was in fact the same.
Whether it were against the hosts of Susa and
Ecbatana, or against " the dog Anubis " and the
Egyptian queen, each battle was the triumph of
Western discipline, religion, virtue, over the tide of
sensuality and superstition which swept onwards
from the unfathomable East.

And thus we come to the point where Virgil
is, in reality, closely identified with the policy of
the Augustan *régime*. Augustus was not himself
a moral hero. But partly fortune, partly wisdom,
partly a certain innate preference for order and
reverence for the gods, had rendered him the only
available representative, not only of the constitution
and the history, but of the morals and religion of
Rome. The leading pre-occupation of his official
life was the restoration of national virtue. It is
hard to trace the success or failure of an attempt
like this among a complex society's conflicting
currents of good and evil. Yet it seems that to his
strenuous insistance on all of morality which

---

[1] Aesch. Pers. 395.　　　　[2] Psyttalea. Pers. 447.

legislation can achieve, we may in some measure ascribe that moonlight of Roman virtue which mingles so long its chastened gentleness with the blaze of the Empire's lurid splendour, the smoke of its foul decay. A reform like this, however, cannot be achieved by a single ruler. And sincere co-operation was hard to find. Papius and Poppæus might pass laws against celibacy. But Papius and Poppæus themselves (as Boissier reminds us) remained obstinately unmarried. Horace might sing of praying to the gods "with our wives and children." But no one was ever less than Horace of a church-goer or a family man. Virgil, on the other hand, was one of those men whose adherence seems to give reality to any project of ethical reform. The candid and serious poet, "than whom," as Horace says, "earth bore no whiter soul," was quickly recognised by Mæcenas as the one writer who could with sincerity sound the praises of antique and ingenuous virtue. The Georgics came to the Roman* world somewhat as the writings of Rousseau came to the French; they might have little apparent influence upon conduct, but they made a new element in the mind of the age, they testified at least to the continued life of pure ideas, to the undying conception of a contented labour, of an unbought and guileless joy.

But this was not yet enough. The spirit of Roman virtue needed to be evoked by a sterner spell. In

the Georgics the land of Italy had for the first time
been impressively presented as a living and organic
whole.   And the idea of Italy's lovely primacy
among all other countries was destined to subsist
and grow.   But it was not yet towards the name of
Italy that the enthusiasm of Virgil's fellow-citizens
most readily went out.   However variously expressed
or shrouded, the religion of the Romans was Rome.
The destiny of the Eternal City is without doubt
the conception which, throughout the long roll of
human history, has come nearest to the unchange-
able and the divine.   It is an idea majestic enough
to inspire worship, and to be the guide of life and
death.   This religion of Rome, in its strictest sense,
has formed no trifling factor in the story of the
Christian Church.   It appears in its strongest and
most unquestioning form in the De Monarchia of
Dante.   It formed a vital part of the creed of the
great Italian who in our own century has risen to
closest communion in thought and deed with the
heroes of his country's past.   But ·nowhere, from
Ennius to Mazzini, has this faith found such expression as in Virgil's Æneid.   All is there.   There
is nothing lacking of noble reminiscence, of high
exhortation, of inspiring prophecy.   Roman virtue
is appealed to through the channel by which alone
it could be reached and could be restored ; it is
renewed by majestic memories and stimulated by
an endless hope.   The Georgics had been the psalm

of Italy, the Æneid was the sacred book of the
Religion of Rome.

It appears, then, that although Virgil doubtless
lent all his weight to the personal government of
Augustus, he neither chose that government in preference to any attainable form of stable freedom,
nor co-operated with it in an unfitting manner, nor
with an unworthy aim. There remains the question
of the deification of Augustus — of the impulse
given by Virgil to that worship of the emperors
which ultimately became so degrading and so cruel
a farce. And here, no doubt, in one passage at
least, Virgil's language is such as modern taste must
condemn. The frigid mythology with which the
first Georgic opens is absolutely bad. It is bad as
Callimachus is bad, and as every other imitation of
Callimachus in Latin literature is bad too. It has,
indeed, little meaning; and what meaning it has
would need an astrologer to decipher. What are
we to make of Tethys and of Proserpine, of Thule
and of Elysium, or of the Scorpion who is willing
to draw in his claws to make room for Augustus in
heaven ? It has, indeed, been ingeniously suggested
that the true point of this strange passage may con-
sist in a veiled but emphatic warning to Augustus
not to assume the title of King,[1] (a title of which,
as in Caligula's case, the Romans were far more
chary than of the less practical ascription of god-

---

[1] G. i. 36-7. The suggestion is Mr. Raper's.

head); and, moreover, that the poet himself subsequently apologises [1] for the unreality of the flattering exordium in which this lesson is concealed. Still, we must regret that any passage in Virgil should require such apology. We cannot help seeing more dignity in the tone of Lucretius, whose only feeling with regard to earthly potentates was vexation at their being too busy to allow him to explain his philosophy to them as fully as he could have wished.[2]

The passages in the Æneid in which Augustus is prospectively deified stand on a different footing. In them he is more or less closely identified with Rome herself; he is represented as we see him in the great allegorical statue of the Vatican, — "Augustus Cæsar leading the Italians on to war, with the Senate and the people and the tutelary gods of Rome,"[3] the creation of that early moment in the empire's history when it seemed as if the conflicting currents of the Commonwealth might run at length in a single channel, and the State be symbolised not unworthily in the man whom she had chosen as her chief. And, indeed, when we consider the proportions which the worship of "Rome and the genius of Augustus" gradually assumed, the earnestness with which it was pressed on by the people in face of what seems to have been the genuine disapproval of the cautious Emperor,

---

[1] G. ii. 45-6.   [2] Lucr. i. 43.   [3] A. viii. 678.

the speed with which it became, without formal change or definite installation, the practical religion of the Roman world,[1] we shall see reason to suppose that this strange form of worship, to which Virgil gave perhaps the earliest, though in part an unconscious expression, was not the birth of a merely meaningless servility, but represented what was in fact a religious reform and a return to the oldest instincts of the Roman people.

The Roman religion, as we first hear of it, shows us an Aryan tradition already strongly modified by the Roman character, by a tone of mind abstract and juristic, rather than creative or joyous. Some of the natural powers whose worship the earliest Romans, in common with the earliest Greeks, had inherited from their Aryan ancestors had already acquired a definite quasi-human personality. These the Roman necessarily accepted as persons, though he added no fresh vividness to the conception of them. But his feeble instinct of anthropomorphism hardly went farther than this; and such deities as he himself created,—such tutelary powers, I should rather say, as he thought might be useful if they

---

[1] See M. Boissier's *Religion Romaine* on all this subject, and especially for an account of the colleges of Augustales, which were the earliest trade-guilds, the earliest representative bodies, the model followed in Christian ecclesiastical organisation, and the first religious bodies on a large scale which admitted all men, without distinction of wealth or birth, to a full share in their privileges and in their control.

happened to exist,—were individualised in the most shadowy manner. They were little more than the sublimated counterparts or correspondences of acts or beings visible here on earth. These deified abstractions were of very various magnitude and dignity, ranging from Minerva, Goddess of Memory, and Janus, God of Opening, down to the crowd of divinities little heard of outside the *Indigitamenta* or handy-book of the Gods, the Goddess of Going Out and the Goddess of Coming In, the God of Silver Money and his father the God of Copper Money, and the God of Speaking Intelligibly, who never made more than a single remark.[1] As the Romans came into contact with other nations, especially with Greece, foreign deities were introduced; but these were identified as far as possible with the Roman deities of similar functions, and did not overthrow the balance of the old *régime*. But as the strange Eastern gods, with their gloomy or frenzied worships, were added to the list this quiet absorption was no longer possible. The Roman Olympus came to resemble a shifting and turbulent Convention, in which now one and now another member,—Dionysus, Isis, Cybele,—rises tumultuously into predominance, and is in turn eclipsed by some newer arrival. This inroad of furious and conflicting superstitions had begun in Virgil's time, and the battle of Actium is for him the defeat of

---

[1] Iterduca, Domiduca, Argentinus, Æsculanus, Aius Locutius.

the "monstrous forms of gods of every birth,"[1] who
would have made their entry with Antony into
Rome.   At the same time it was hard to suggest an
effective antidote for these degrading worships.   The
gods, so to speak, of the middle period—Jupiter and
Juno and the like, with a Greek personality super-
added to their more abstract significance—had not
vitality enough to expel the intruders from their
domain.   It was necessary to fall back upon a more
thoroughly national and primitive conception, and
to deify once more the abstraction of the one
earthly existence whose greatness was overwhelm-
ingly evident—the power of Rome.   The "Fortune
of the City," or *Roma* herself enthroned with the
insignia of a Goddess, was the only queen who
could overrule at once the epidemic fanaticisms of
Rome and the localised cults of the provinces, and
be the veritable mistress of heaven.

Nor was even she enough.   Through the abstractions of the old Roman religion there had always
run a thread of more intimate and personal worship.
Not only had each action and each object its spiritual
counterpart, but each man as well.   The nature of
these Lares was somewhat vaguely and obscurely
conceived, but the dominant idea seems to have
been that they acted as the tutelary genii of men
during life, and after death became identical with
their immortal part.   The Roman worship of an-

[1] A. viii. 698.

cestors was indeed of a different kind from the hero-
worship of the Greeks. It dwelt less on the idea
of superhuman help than on the idea of family
continuity. The Romans had not the faith which
bade the Locrians leave a place always open in their
battle-ranks for the Oïlean Ajax to fill unseen; but
they testified by daily offering and daily prayer to
their conviction of an immanent and familiar presence which turned the home itself into a never-
vacant shrine. They asked no oracle from "Amphiaraus beneath the earth;" but the images of his
curule ancestors gathered round about the dead
Fabius in the market-place, and welcomed him in
silence as he joined the majority of his kin. It is
this spirit of piety which the plot of the Æneid is
designed to illustrate and to foster. Æneas has
no wish to conquer Latium. He enters it merely
because he is divinely instructed that it is in Italy,
the original home of his race, that he must continue
the worship of his own progenitor Assaracus and of
the tutelary gods of Troy. This point achieved he
asks for nothing more. He introduces the worship
of Assaracus; but, it must be added, Assaracus is
never heard of again. So remote and legendary a
personage could not become the binding link of the
Roman people. Nor had the Roman commonwealth
ever yet stood in such a relation to any single family
as to permit the identification of their private Lares
with the Lares Præstites of the city of Rome. But

the case was altered now. One family had risen to an isolated pre - eminence which no Roman had attained before. And by a singular chance this same family combined a legendary with an actual primacy. Augustus was at once the representative of Assaracus and the master of the Roman world. The Lares of Augustus were at once identical in a certain sense with Augustus himself, and with the public Penates worshipped immemorially in their chapel in the heart of the city. And if, as is no doubt the case, the worship of Roma and the Lares augusti could claim in Virgil its half-unconscious prophet, we may reply that this worship, however afterwards debased, was in its origin and essence neither novel nor servile, but national and antique; and that until the rise of Christianity, towards which Virgil stands in a yet more singular anticipatory relation, it would have been hard to say what other form of religion could at once have satisfied the ancient instincts and bound together the remote extremities of the Roman world.

The relation of Virgil to Christianity, to which we now come, is an unexpectedly complex matter. To understand it clearly, we must attempt to disentangle some of the threads of religious emotion and belief which intertwine in varying proportions throughout his successive poems.

"Reared among the woods and thickets," an Italian country child, the counterpart of Words-

worth in the union of spiritual aspiration with rustic
simplicity in which his early years were spent,
Virgil, like Wordsworth, seemed singled out as the
poet and priest of nature. And directly imitated
as his Eclogues are from Theocritus, a closer investi-
gation reveals the essential differences between the
nature of the two poets. The idylls of Theocritus
are glowing descriptions of pastoral life, written by
a man who lives and enjoys that life, and cares for
no other ideal. The Eclogues of Virgil have less of
consistency, but they have more of purpose. They
are an advocacy, none the less impassioned because
indirect, of the charm of scenery and simple pleasures
addressed to a society leading a life as remote from
nature as the life of the French court in the days of
Rousseau. Theocritus, delighting in everything connected with rural life, loves to paint with vigour
even its least dignified scenes. Virgil—whom the
Neapolitans called the Maid, and who shrank aside
when any one looked at him—is grotesquely artificial
when he attempts to render the coarse *badinage* of
country clowns. On the other hand, where the
emotion in Theocritus is pure and worthy, Virgil is
found at his side, with so delicate a reproduction of
his effects, that it is sometimes hard to say whether
the Greek or the Latin passage seems the more
spontaneous and exquisite.[1] And there is a whole
region of higher emotions in which the Latin poet is

---

[1] Compare E. viii. 37, with Theocr. xi. 25.

alone. All Virgil's own are those sudden touches of exalted friendship,[1] of exquisite tenderness,[2] of the sadness and the mystery of love,[3] which seem to murmur amid the bright flow of his pastoral poetry of the deep source from whence it springs, as his own Eridanus had his fountain in Paradise and the underworld.[4] All Virgil's own, too, is the comprehending vision, the inward eye which looks back through all man's wars and tumult to the new-created mountains[5] and the primal spring,[6] and that "wise passiveness" to which nature loves to offer her consolation, which fills so often the interspace between faiths decayed and faiths re-risen with a

---

[1] *e.g.* E. vi. 64. The whole of the tenth eclogue is an exquisite example of the half-tender, half-sportive sympathy by which one friend can best strengthen another in the heart's lesser troubles, and the blank when light loves have flown. The delicate humour of this eclogue has perplexed the German commentators, who suggest (1) either that Virgil meant it as a parody on the fifth eclogue, or (2) that Gallus was in fact dead when it was written, and that the poem,—ostensibly composed to console him for being jilted by an actress,—was, in reality, intended as a sort of funeral psalm. I may notice here the improbability of the story that Virgil altered the end of the Fourth Georgic, omitting a panegyric on Gallus after Gallus' disgrace and death. The Georgics were published B.C. 29, and Gallus died B.C. 26. It is hard to believe that a long passage, constituting the conclusion and crown of the most popular and best known poem that had ever appeared in Rome, and deriving added interest from the political scandal involved, should, after being three years before the public, have perished so utterly that not a line, not a fragment of a line, not an allusion to the passage, should anywhere remain.

[2] *e.g.* E. iv. 60.   [3] *e.g.* E. viii. 47.   [4] A. vi. 658.
[5] E. vi. 40.   [6] G. ii. 338.

tranquillised abeyance of doubt and fear. " Pan
and old Silvanus and the sister nymphs ; " Silenus
keeping the shepherds spell-bound till twilight with
his cosmic song ; Proteus uttering his unwilling
oracles upon the solitary shore ; Clymene singing of
love in the caverned water-world amid the rivers'
roaring flow ;—what are all these but aspects and
images of that great mother who has for all her
children a message which sometimes seems only
the sweeter because its meaning can be so dimly
known ?

Peculiar to Virgil, too, is that tone of expecta-
tion which recurs again and again to the hope of
some approaching union of mankind beneath a juster
heaven, which bids the shepherd look no longer on
the old stars with worn-out promises, but on a star
new-risen and more benign ; which tells in that
mystical poem to which scholars know no key, how
the pure and stainless shepherd dies and is raised
to heaven, and begins from thence a gentle sway
which forbids alike the wild beast's ravin and the
hunter's cruel guile.[1]

> " O great good news thro' all the woods that ran !
> O psalm and praise of shepherds and of Pan !
> The hills unshorn to heaven their voices fling ;
> Desert and wilderness rejoice and sing ;
> ' A god he is ! a god we guessed him then !
> Peace on the earth he sends and joy to men.' "

---

[1] E. v. 58.

But it is, of course, the Fourth, or Messianic Eclogue (known to the English reader in Pope's paraphrase, *Ye nymphs of Solyma, begin the song*), which has formed the principal point of union between Virgil and the new faith. In every age of Christianity, from Augustine to Abelard, from the Christmas sermon of Pope Innocent III. to the Prælectiones Academicæ of the late Mr. Keble, divines and fathers of the Church have asserted the inspiration, and claimed the prophecies of this marvellous poem. It was on the strength of this poem that Virgil's likeness was set among the carven seers in the Cathedral of Zamora. It was on the strength of this poem that in the Cathedrals of Limoges and Rheims the Christmas appeal was made : " O Maro, prophet of the Gentiles, bear thou thy witness unto Christ ; " and the stately semblance of the Roman gave answer in the words which tell how " the new progeny has descended from heaven on high." The prophecy can claim œcumenical acceptance, regenerative efficacy. The poet Statius, the martyr Secundianus, were said to have been made Christians by its perusal. And at the supreme moment of the transference and reconstruction of the civil and spiritual authority of the earth, the Emperor Constantine in his oration, "inscribed to the Assembly of Saints and dedicated to the Church of God," commented on this poem in a Greek version, as forming a link between the old and the new faiths,

as explaining the change of form, and justifying the
historical continuity, of the religion of the civilised
world.

And there is nothing in this which need either
surprise or shock us.[1]　For, in reality, the link between Virgil and Christianity depended not on a

[1] There is, no doubt, a startling antithesis between the real and
the supposed object of Virgil's prophecy.　For there can surely be
little doubt (as Bishop Louth, Boissier, etc., have argued) that the
Fourth Eclogue was written in anticipation of the birth of the
child of Augustus (then Octavianus) and Scribonia—the notorious
Julia, born B.C. 39, shortly after the peace of Brundusium.　The
words "te consule" applied to Pollio make it most unlikely that he
was the child's *father*.　On the other hand, it would have been
quite in keeping with Virgil's stately courtesy to address to Pollio,
Antony's representative and Virgil's friend, a congratulatory poem
on the birth in his consulship of a child to Augustus, with whom
Antony had just been reconciled.　Virgil was from the first one of
the most ardent supporters of Augustus, and though the young heir
of Cæsar was not as yet clearly the first man in Rome, still, the
prestige of the Julian family alone could make the expressions of
the poem seem other than extravagant.　Virgil no doubt desired
to associate Pollio as closely as possible with the hopes of the
Roman commonwealth.　But to speak of "a world at peace
through Pollio's virtue" would have been no less than absurd.
Moreover, the phrase, "thy Apollo is in the ascendant now,"
points clearly to Augustus, whose patron Apollo was.　The reason
why the riddle was not explained is obvious.　The expected child
turned out to be a girl—and a girl who perhaps gave rise to more
scandal than any other member of her sex.　It is singular that the
embarrassing failure of the prediction at the time has been the
source of its extraordinary reputation afterwards, when the horo-
scope composed for Julia was fulfilled in Jesus Christ.　Like the
arrow of Acestes (A. v. 520), the prophecy seemed to consume away
in the clouds and burn itself into empty air—

"Till days far off its mighty meaning knew,
　And seers long after sang the presage true."

misapplied prediction but on a moral sequence, a
spiritual conformity.   There was a time when both
the apologists and the adversaries of Christianity
were disposed to ignore its connection with preced-
ing faiths.   Exaggerated pictures of its miraculous
diffusion were met by the sneers of Gibbon at the
contagious spread of superstitions among the ruins
of a wiser world.   The tone of both parties has
altered as historical criticism has advanced.   It is
recognised that it is only " in the fulness of time "
that a great religious change can come; that men's
minds must be prepared for new convictions by a
need which has been deeply felt, and a habit of
thought which has been slowly acquired.   And in
Virgil's time, as has already been said, the old
dogmas were tending to disappear.   But while in
the lower minds they were corrupting into superstition, in the higher they were evaporating into a
clearer air.   The spiritual element was beginning
to assert itself over the ceremonial.   Instincts of
catholic charity were beginning to put to shame the
tribal narrowness of the older faith.   Philosophy
was issuing from the lecture-room into the forum
and the street.

And thus it is that Virgil's poems lie at the
watershed of religions.   Filled as they are with
Roman rites and Roman tradition, they contain also
another element, gentler, holier, till then almost
unknown ; a change has passed over them like the

change which passes over a Norwegian midnight when the rose of evening becomes silently the rose of dawn.

It is strange to trace the alternate attraction and repulsion which the early Christians felt towards Virgil. Sometimes they allegorised the Æneid into a kind of Siege of Man-soul, in which the fall, the temptations, the deliverance of man, are recorded in a figure. Sometimes they compiled Christianised centos from his poems,—works which obtained such authority that Pope Gelasius found it necessary to pronounce *ex cathedrâ* that they formed no part of the canon of Scripture. Sometimes, as in Augustine, we watch the conflict in a higher air; we see the ascetic absorption in the new faith at war with the truer instinct, which warns him that all noble emotions are in reality mutually supporting, and that we debase instead of ennobling our devotion to one supreme ideal if we shrink from recognising the goodness and greatness of ideals which are not to us so dear. But even in the wild legends which in the Middle Ages cluster so thickly round the name of Virgil, even in the distorted fancies of the hamlet or the cloister, we can discern some glimmering perception of an actual truth. It is not true, as the Spanish legend tells us, that "Virgil's eyes first saw the star of Bethlehem;" but it is true that in none more fully than in him is found that temper which offers all worldly wealth, all human learning,

at the feet of Purity, and for the knowledge of
Truth.   It is not true that Virgil was a magician;
that he clove the rock; that he wrought a gigantic
figure which struck a note of warning at the far-
seen onset of tumult or of war; but it is true that
he was one of those who *"like giants stand, to
sentinel enchanted land,"* whose high thoughts have
caught and reflect the radiance of some mysterious
and unrisen day.

Although the interest which subsequent ages
have taken in the religion of Virgil has turned
mainly upon his relation to Christianity, he would
himself, of course, have judged in another light the
growth of his inward being.   A celebrated passage
in the Georgics has revealed to us his mood of mind
in a decisive hour.   To understand it we must refer
to the strongest influence which his youth was
destined to undergo.   When Virgil was on the
threshold of life a poem was published which,
perhaps, of all single monuments of Roman genius,
conveys to us the most penetrating conception of
the irresistible force of Rome.   There is no need to
deck Lucretius with any attributes not his own.
We may grant that his poetry is often uncouth, his
science confused, his conception of human existence
steeped in a lurid gloom.   But no voice like his has
ever proclaimed the nothingness of "momentary
man," no prophet so convincing has ever thundered
in our ears the appalling Gospel of Death.   Few

minds, perhaps, that were not stiffly cased in fore-
gone conclusions have ever met the storm of his
passionate eloquence without bending before the
blast, without doubting for an hour of their inmost
instincts, and half believing that " as we felt no woe
in times long gone, when from all the earth to battle
the Carthaginians came," so now it may be man's
best and only hope to quench in annihilation his
unsated longings and his deep despair.

On Virgil's nature, disposed at once to vague
sadness and to profound inquiry, the six books on
the Nature of Things produced their maximum
effect. Alike in his thought and language we see
the Lucretian influence mingling with that spirit of
natural religion which seems to have been his own
earliest bent ; and at last, in the passage above referred to,[1] he pauses between the two hypotheses,
each alike incapable of proof ; that which assumes
that because we see in nature an impersonal order,
therefore there is no more to see, and that which
assumes that because we feel within us a living
spirit, the universe, too, lives around us and breathes
with the divine.

" If thou thy secrets grudge me, nor assign
  So high a lore to such a heart as mine,—
  Still, Nature, let me still thy beauty know,
  Love the clear streams that thro' thy valleys flow,

---

[1] G. ii. 490. The last two lines of the version here given
merely summarise a passage too long for quotation.

To many a forest lawn that love proclaim,
Breathe the full soul, and make an end of fame !
Ah me, Spercheos ! oh to watch alway
On Taygeta the Spartan girls at play !
Or cool in Hæmus' gloom to feel me laid,
Deep in his branching solitudes of shade !
　　Happy the man whose steadfast eye surveys
The whole world's truth, its hidden works and ways,—
Happy, who thus beneath his feet has thrown
All fears and fates, and Hell's insatiate moan !—
Blest, too, were he the sister nymphs who knew,
Pan, and Sylvanus, and the sylvan crew ;—
On kings and crowds his careless glance he flings,
And scorns the treacheries of crowds and kings ;
Far north the leaguered hordes are hovering dim ;
Danube and Dacian have no dread for him ;
No shock of laws can fright his steadfast home,
Nor realms in ruin nor all the fates of Rome.
Round him no glare of envied wealth is shed,
From him no piteous beggar prays for bread ;
Earth, Earth herself the unstinted gift will give,
Her trustful children need but reap and live ;
She hath man's peace 'mid all the worldly stir,
One with himself he is, if one with her."

And henceforth without fanatical blindness, but
with a slow deliberate fervour, he elects to act upon
the latter opinion ; and from this time we find little
trace of the influence of Lucretius in his poems,
except it may be some quickening of that delight
in the hidden things of nature which makes the
world's creation Iopas',[1] as it was Silenus'[2] song ;

---

[1] A. i. 743.　　　　　　　　　　[2] E. vi. 31

some deepening of that mournful wonder with which he regards the contrast between the hopes and fates of men.

And is there, then, anything in Virgil's creed more definite than this vague spirituality ? Is there any moral government of the world of which he can speak to us from the heart ? If so, it is not in connection with the old gods of Rome, for they have lost their individual life. They are no longer like those gods of Homer's, who "sat on the brow of Callicolone," awful in their mingling of aloofness and reality, of terror and subduing charm. Jove's frowns, Cytherea's caresses, in the Æneid assume alike an air of frigid routine. And in the unfinished later books the references to the heavenly council-board are of so curt and formal a character that they can deceive no one. It is as if the poet felt bound to say, "that the gods had taken the matter into their most serious consideration,"[1] "that it was with great regret that the gods found themselves unable to concede a longer term of existence to the Daunian hero,"[2] while all the time he was well aware that the gods had never been consulted in the matter at all.

And even that more real and comprehensive religion of Rome, the inspiring belief in the destinies of the Eternal City, lacked that which is lacking to all such religions, whether their object be one city

---

[1] A. xii. 843.   [2] A. xii. 725.

only or the whole corporate commonwealth of men.
There was no place in it for individual recompense;
it left unanswered the imperious demand of the
moral sense that not one sentient soul shall be
created to agony that others may be blest. Such
faiths may inspire ceremonial, may prompt to action,
but they cannot justify the ways of God to man, nor
satisfy or control the heart.

It is well known that in the central passage of
the Æneid, the speech of the shade of Anchises to
Æneas in Elysium,[1] Virgil has abruptly relinquished
his efforts to revive or harmonise legendary beliefs,
and has propounded an answer to the riddle of the
universe in an unexpectedly definite form. It would
be interesting to trace the elements of Stoic, Platonic,
Pythagorean thought which combine in this remarkable passage. But such an inquiry would be beyond
our present scope, and must in any case rest largely
upon conjecture, for Virgil, who seems to have been
working upon this exposition till the last,[2] and who
meant, as we know, to devote to philosophy the rest
of his life after the completion of the Æneid, has
given us no indication of the process by which he
reached these results—results singular as contrasting
so widely with the official religion of which he was
in some sort the representative, yet which may

---

[1] A. vi. 724-755.

[2] See A. vi. 743-7, as indicating that the arrangement of this
passage is incomplete.

surprise us less when we consider their close coincidence with the independent conclusions of many
thinkers of ancient and modern times. A brief
description of the passage referred to will fitly conclude the present essay.

Æneas, warned of Anchises in a vision, has
penetrated the underworld to consult his father's
shade. He finds Anchises surrounded by an in-
numerable multitude of souls, who congregate on
Lethe's shore. His father tells him that these souls
are drinking the waters of oblivion, and will then
return to live again on earth. Æneas is astonished
at this, and the form of the question which he
asks [1] is in itself highly significant. Compared, for
example, with the famous contrast which the
Homeric Achilles draws between even the poorest
life on happy earth and the forlorn kingship of the
shades, it indicates that a change has taken place
which of all speculative changes is perhaps the most
important, that the ideal has been shifted from the
visible to the invisible, from the material to the
spiritual world—

"O father, must I deem that souls can pray
  Hence to turn backward to the worldly day?
  Change for that weight of flesh these forms more fair,
  For that sun's sheen this paradisal air?"

The speech of Anchises in answer is in a certain
sense the most Virgilian passage in Virgil. All his

---

[1] A. vi. 719.

characteristics appear in it in their highest intensity; the pregnant allusiveness, the oracular concentration, the profound complexity, and through them all that unearthly march of song, that "Elysian beauty, melancholy grace," which made him the one fit master for that other soul whom he "*mise dentro alle segrete cose*," to whom in face of purgatory's fiercest fire [1] he promised the reward of constancy, and spoke of the redemptions of love.

The translator may well hesitate before such a passage as this. But as a knowledge of the Theodicy here unfolded is absolutely necessary to the English reader who would understand Virgil aright, some version shall be given here—

" One Life through all the immense creation runs,
   One Spirit is the moon's, the sea's, the sun's ;
   All forms in the air that fly, on the earth that creep,
   And the unknown nameless monsters of the deep,—
   Each breathing thing obeys one Mind's control,
   And in all substance is a single Soul.
   First to each seed a fiery force is given ;
   And every creature was begot in heaven ;
   Only their flight must hateful flesh delay
   And gross limbs moribund and cumbering clay.
   So from that hindering prison and night forlorn
   Thy hopes and fears, thy joys and woes are born,
   Who only seest, till death dispart thy gloom,
   The true world glow through crannies of a tomb.

---

[1] Purg. xxvii. 20

Nor all at once thine ancient ills decay,
Nor quite with death thy plagues are purged away ;
In wondrous wise hath the iron entered in,
And through and through thee is a stain of sin ;
Which yet again in wondrous wise must be
Cleansed of the fire, abolished in the sea ;
Ay, thro' and thro' that soul unclothed must go
Such spirit-winds as where they list will blow ;—
O hovering many an age ! for ages bare,
Void in the void and impotent in air !
　　Then, since his sins unshriven the sinner wait,
And to each soul that soul herself is Fate,
Few to heaven's many mansions straight are sped
(Past without blame that Judgment of the dead),
The most shall mourn till tarrying Time hath wrought
The extreme deliverance of the airy thought,—
Hath left unsoiled by fear or foul desire
The spirit's self, the elemental fire.
　　And last to Lethe's stream on the ordered day
These all God summoneth in great array ;
Who from that draught reborn, no more shall know
Memory of past or dread of destined woe,
But all shall there the ancient pain forgive,
Forget their life, and will again to live."

The shade of Anchises is silent here. But let us add some lines from the Georgics,[1] in which Virgil carries these souls yet farther, and to the term of their wondrous way—

" Then since from God those lesser lives began,
　　And the eager spirits entered into man,

---

[1] G. iv. 223.

To God again the enfranchised soul must tend,
He is her home, her Author is her End ;
No death is hers ; when earthly eyes grow dim
Starlike she soars and Godlike melts in Him."

But why must we recur to an earlier poem for the consummation which was most of all needed here ? and why, at the end of the sixth book, has the poet struck that last strange note of doubt and discord, dismissing Æneas from the shades by the deluding Ivory Gate, proclaiming, as it were, like Plato, his Theodicy as " neither false nor true," as a dream among dreams that wander and " visions unbelievable and fair ?" We turn, like Dante, in hope of the wise guide's reply. But he has left us at last alone.[1] He has led us to the region " where of himself he can see no more ;"[2] we must expect from him no longer " either word or sign." He parts from us in the " antelucan splendour," and at the gate of heaven, at the very moment when a hundred angels sing aloud with fuller meaning his own words of solemn welcome and unforgetful love.[3] To Dante all the glory of paradise could not avail to keep his eyes from scorching tears at his " sweetest father's " sad withdrawal and uncompleted way :— we too, perhaps, may feel mournfully the lot of man as we think of him on whose yearning spirit all revelation that nature, or that science, or that faith

---

[1] Purg. xxx. 49.   [2] Purg. xxvii. 129, 139.
[3] Purg. xxx. 21.

could show, fell only as day's last glory on the
fading vision of the Carthaginian queen [1]—

" For thrice she turned, and thrice had fain dispread
  Her dying arms to lift her dying head ;
  Thrice in high heaven, with dimmed eyes wandering
    wide,
  She sought the light, and found the light, and sighed."

So was it with those who by themselves should
not be made perfect ; they differed from the saints
of Christendom not so much in the emotion which
they offered as in the emotion with which they were
repaid ; it was elevation but it was not ecstasy ; it
came to them not as hope but as calm. What
touch of unattainable holiness was lacking for their
reception into Dante's Paradisal Rose ? what ardour
of love was still unknown to them which should
have been their foretaste and their pledge of heaven ?
" Dark night enwraps their heads with hovering
gloom," and from this man, their solitary rearguard,
and on the very confines of the day, we can part
only in words of such sad reverence as salute in his
own song that last and most divinely glorified of the
inhabitants of the underworld [2]—

" Give, give me lilies ; thick the flowers be laid
  To greet that mighty, melancholy shade ;
  With such poor gifts let me his praise maintain,
  And mourn with useless tears, and crown in vain."

[1] A. iv. 690.   [2] A. vi. 883.

Ἄγου δέ μ', ὦ Ζεῦ, καὶ σύγ' ἡ Πεπρωμένη,
ὅποι ποθ'ὑμῖν εἰμὶ διατεταγμένος·
ὡς ἔψομαί γ' ἄοκνος· ἢν δὲ μὴ θέλω,
κακὸς γενόμενος οὐδὲν ἧττον ἔψομαι.

CLEANTHES.

SOME apology may seem to be due from one who ventures to treat once again of Marcus Aurelius Antoninus. Few characters in history have been oftener or more ably discussed during the present age, an age whose high aims and uncertain creed have found at once impulse and sympathy in the meditations of the crowned philosopher. And, finally, the most subtle and attractive of living historians has closed his strange portrait-gallery with this majestic figure, accounting that the sun of Christianity was not fully risen till it had seen the paling of the old world's last and purest star.

The subject has lost, no doubt, its literary freshness, but its moral and philosophical significance is still unexhausted. Even an increased interest, indeed, may be felt at the present time in considering the relations which the philosophy of Marcus bears either to ancient or to modern religious thought. For he has been made, as it were, the saint and exemplar of Agnosticism, the type of all such virtue and wisdom as modern criticism can allow to be sound or permanent. It will be the object of the following essay to suggest some reflections on the position thus assigned to him, dwelling only incidentally, and as briefly as may be consistent with clearness, on the more familiar aspects of his opinions and his career.

Character and circumstances, rather than talent or originality, give to the thoughts of Marcus Aurelius their especial value and charm. And although the scanty notices of his life which have come down to us have now been often repeated, it seems necessary to allude to some of the more characteristic of them if we would understand the spiritual outlook of one who is not a closet-philosopher moralising *in vacuo*, but the son of Pius, the father of Commodus, the master of a declining world.

The earliest statue which we know of Marcus represents him as a youth offering sacrifice. The earliest story of him, before his adoption into the Imperial family, is of his initiation, at eight years old, as a Salian priest of Mars, when the crowns flung by the other priests fell here and there around the recumbent statue, but the crown which young Marcus threw to him lit and rested on the war-

god's head.   The boy-priest, we are told, could soon
conduct all the ceremonies of the Salian cult without
the usual prompter, for he served in all its offices,
and knew all its hymns by heart.   And it well became him thus to begin by exhibiting the characteristic piety of a child;—who passes in his growing
years through the forms of worship, as of thought,
which have satisfied his remote forefathers, and
ripens himself for his adult philosophies with the
consecrated tradition of the past.

Our next glimpse is of the boy growing into
manhood in the household of his adopted father,
Antoninus Pius, whom he is already destined to
succeed on the Imperial throne.   One of the lessons
for which Marcus afterwards revered his father's
memory was the lesson of simplicity maintained in
the palace of princes, " far removed from the habits
of the rich."   The correspondence between the Imperial boy and his tutor, Fronto, shows us how pronounced this simplicity was, and casts a curious
side-light on the power of the Roman Emperor, who
can impress his own individuality with so uncom-
promising a hand not only on the affairs of the
empire, but on the personal habits of his court and
entourage.   In the modern world the more absolute
a monarch is in one way, the more is he in another
way fettered and constrained ; for his absolutism
relies on an artificial prestige which can dispense
with no means of impressing the vulgar mind.   And

in freer countries there is always a set of necessary persons, an habitual tone of manners, which the sovereign cannot afford to ignore. A George III. may lead a frugal family life, but he is forced to conciliate and consort with social leaders of habits quite opposite to his own. A William IV. who fails to do this adequately is pronounced to be " not in society." Antoninus Pius might certainly have been said to be "out of society," but that there was no society for him to be in except his own. The " optimates," whose opinion Cicero treats as the acknowledged standard— a group of notables enjoying social as well as official pre-eminence—had practically ceased to exist. Even the Senate, whose dignity the Antonines so sedu- lously cherished, consisted mainly of new and low- born men. Everything depended on the individual tastes of the ruler. Play-actors were at the head of society under Nero, spies under Domitian, philoso- phers under the Antonines.

The letters of the young Marcus to Fronto are very much such letters as might be written at the pre- sent day by the home-taught son of an English squire to a private tutor to whom he was much attached. They are, however, more effusive than an English style allows, and although Marcus in his youth was a suc- cessful athlete, they seldom refer to games or hunting. I translate one of them as a specimen of the rest :—

" I slept late this morning on account of my cold, but it is better. From five in the morning till nine I partly read Cato on Agriculture, and partly wrote, not quite such rubbish as yesterday. Then I greeted my father, and then soothed my throat with honey-water without absolutely gargling. Then I attended my father as he offered sacrifice. Then to breakfast. What do you think I ate? only a little bread, though I saw the others devouring beans, onions, and sardines! Then we went out to the vintage, and got hot and merry, but left a few grapes still hanging, as the old poet says, 'atop on the topmost bough.' At noon we got home again; I worked a little, but it was not much good. Then I chatted a long time with my mother as she sat on her bed. My conversation consisted of, 'What do you suppose my Fronto is doing at this moment?' to which she answered, 'And my Gratia, what is she doing?' and then I, 'And our little birdie, Gratia the less?' And while we were talking and quarrelling as to which of us loved all of you the best, the gong sounded, which meant that my father had gone across to the bath. So we bathed and dined in the oil-press room. I don't mean that we bathed in the press-room; but we bathed and then dined, and amused ourselves with listening to the peasants' banter. And now that I am in my own room again, before I roll over and snore, I am fulfilling my promise and giving an account of my day to my dear tutor; and if I could love him better than I do I would consent to miss him even more than I miss him now. Take care of yourself, my best and dearest Fronto, wherever you are. The fact is that I love you, and you are far away."

Among the few hints which the correspondence contains of the pupil's rank is one curiously characteristic of his times and his destiny. Tutor and pupil, it seems, were in the habit of sending to each other " hypotheses," or imaginary cases, for the sake of practice in dealing with embarrassing circumstances as they arose. Marcus puts to Fronto the following " hard case " : " A Roman consul at the public games changes his consular dress for a gladiator's, and kills a lion in the amphitheatre before the assembled people. What is to be done to him ? " The puzzled Fronto contents himself with replying that such a thing could not possibly happen. But the boy's ·prevision was true. A generation later this very thing was done by a man who was not only a Roman consul, but a Roman Emperor, and the son of Marcus himself.

These were Marcus' happiest days. The companionship of Pius was a school of all the virtues. His domestic life with Faustina, if we are to believe contemporary letters rather than the scandal of the next century, was, at first at any rate, a model of happiness and peace. Marcus was already forty years old when Pius died. The nineteen years which remained to him were mainly occupied in driving back Germanic peoples from the northern frontiers of the empire. This labour was interrupted in A.D. 175 by the revolt of Avidius Cassius, an event which Marcus employed as a great occasion for magnanimity. The story is one which some dramatist might well seize upon, and show, with a

truer groundwork than Corneille in *Cinna*, how impossible is resentment to the philosophic soul.   But
the moment in these latter years which may be
selected as most characteristic was perhaps that of
the departure of Marcus to Germany in A.D. 178 for
his last and sternest war.   That great irruption of
the Marcomanni was compared by subsequent historians to the invasion of Hannibal.   It was in fact,
and it was dimly felt to be, the beginning of the
end.   The terrified Romans resorted to every expedi-
ent which could attract the favour of heaven or
fortify the spirit of man.   The Emperor threw a
blood-stained spear from the temple of Mars towards
the unknown North, invoking thus for the last time
in antique fashion the tutelary divinity of Rome.
The images of all the gods were laid on couches in
the sight of men, and that holy banquet was set
before them which constituted their worshippers'
most solemn appeal.   But no sacrifices henceforth
were to be for long effectual, nor omens favourable
again ; they could only show the " Roman peace "
no longer sacred, the "Roman world " no longer
stretching " past the sun's year-long way," but
Janus' temple-doors for ever open, and Terminus
receding upon Rome.   Many new rites were also
performed, many foreign gods were approached with
strange expiations.   But the strangest feature in
this religious revival lay in an act of the Emperor
himself.   He was entreated, says Vulcatius, to give

a parting address to his subjects before he set out
into the wilderness of the north ; and for three
days he expounded his philosophy to the people of
Rome.　The anecdote is a strange one, but hardly in
itself improbable.　It accords so well with Marcus'
trust in the power of reason, his belief in the duty
of laying the truth before men !　One can imagine
the sincere gaze, such as his coins show to us ; the
hand, as in the great equestrian statue of the Capitol, uplifted, as though to bless ; the countenance
controlled, as his biographers tell us, to exhibit
neither joy nor pain ; the voice and diction, not
loud nor striking, but grave and clear, as he bade
his hearers " reverence the dæmon within them,"
and " pass from one unselfish action to another,
with memory of God."　Like the fabled Arthur,
he was, as it were, the conscience amid the warring
passions of his knights ; like Arthur, he was himself going forth to meet " death, or he knew not
what mysterious doom."

For indeed his last years are lost in darkness.
A few anecdotes tell of his failing body and resolute
will ; a few bas-reliefs give in fragments a confused
story of the wilderness and of war.　We see marshes
and forests, bridges and battles, captive Sarmatians
brought to judgment, and Marcus still with his hand
uplifted as though bestowing pardon or grace.

The region in which these last years were spent
is to this day one of the most melancholy in Europe.

The forces of nature run to waste without use or beauty. The great Danube spreads himself languidly between uncertain shores. As it was in the days of Marcus so is it now; the traveller from Vienna eastward still sees the white mist cling to the desolate river-terraces, the clouds of wild-fowl swoop and settle among the reedy islands, and along the bays and promontories of the brimming stream.

But over these years hung a shadow darker than could be cast by any visible foe. Plague had become endemic in the Roman world. The pestilence brought from Asia by Verus in A.D. 166 had not yet abated; it had destroyed already (as it would seem) half the population of the Empire; it was achieving its right to be considered by careful historians as the most terrible calamity which has ever fallen upon men. Destined, as it were, to sever race from race and era from era, the plague struck its last blow against the Roman people upon the person of the Emperor himself. He died in the camp, alone. "Why weep for me," were his last words of stern self-suppression, "and not think rather of the pestilence, and of the death of all?"

When the news of his death reached Rome few tears, we are told, were shed. For it seemed to the people that Marcus, like Marcellus, had been but lent to the Roman race; it was natural that he should pass back again from the wilderness to his celestial home. Before the official honours had been

paid to him the Senate and people by acclamation
at his funeral saluted him as " The Propitious God."
No one, says the chronicler, thought of him as
Emperor any more ; but the young men called on
" Marcus, my father," the men of middle age on
" Marcus, my brother," the old men on " Marcus,
my son." *Homo homini deus est, si suum officium
sciat*—and it may well be that those who thus honoured and thus lamented him had never known a
truer son or brother, father or god.

It does not fall within the scope of this essay to
enumerate in detail the measures by which Marcus
had earned the gratitude of the Empire.   But it is
important to remember that neither war nor philosophy had impaired his activity as an administrator.
Politically his reign, like that of Pius, was remarkable for his respectful treatment of the senatorial
order.   Instead of regarding senators as the natural
objects of imperial jealousy, or prey of imperial
avarice, he endeavoured by all means to raise their
dignity and consideration.   Some of them he employed as a kind of privy council, others as governors
of cities.   When at Rome he attended every meeting
of the Senate ; and even when absent in Campania
he would travel back expressly to be present at any
important debate ; nor did he ever leave the council-
hall till the sitting was adjourned.

While Marcus thus attempted to revive a respon-
sible upper class, he was far from neglecting the

interests of the poor. He developed the scheme
of state nurture and education for needy free-born
children which the Flavian emperors had begun.
He reformed the local government of Italy, and
made more careful provision against the recurring
danger of scarcity. He instituted the " tutelary
prætorship" which was to watch over the rights of
orphans — a class often unjustly treated at Rome.
And he fostered and supervised that great development of civil and criminal law which, under the
Antonines, was steadily giving protection to the
minor, justice to the woman, rights to the slave, and
transforming the stern maxims of Roman procedure
into a fit basis for the jurisprudence of the modern
world.

But indeed the true life and influence of Marcus
had scarcely yet begun. In his case, as in many
others, it was not the main occupation, the osten-
sible business of his life, which proved to have the
most enduring value. His most effective hours were
not those spent in his long adjudications, his cease-
less battles, his strenuous ordering of the concerns
of the Roman world. Rather they were the hours
of solitude and sadness, when, " among the Quadi,"
" on the Granua," " at Carnuntum," he consoled his
lonely spirit by jotting down in fragmentary sen-
tences the principles which were his guide through
life. The little volume was preserved by some for-
tunate accident. For many centuries it was accounted

as a kind of curiosity of literature—as heading the brief list of the writings of kings. From time to time some earnest spirit discovered that the help given by the little book was of surer quality than he could find in many a volume which promised more. One and another student was moved to translate it—from old Gataker of Rotherhithe, completing the work in his seventy-eighth year, as his best preparation for death, to "Cardinal Francis Barberini the elder, who dedicated the translation to his soul, in order to make it redder than his purple at the sight of the virtues of this Gentile."[1] But the complete success of the book was reserved for the present century. I will quote one passage only as showing the position which it has taken among some schools of modern thought—a passage in which a writer celebrated for his nice distinctions and balanced praise has spoken of the *Meditations* in terms of more unmixed eulogy than he has ever bestowed elsewhere :—

"Véritable Evangile éternel," says M. Renan, "le livre des Pensées ne vieillira jamais, car il n'affirme aucun dogme. L'Evangile a vieilli en certaines parties; la science ne permet plus d'admettre la naïve conception du surnaturel qui en fait la base. Le surnaturel n'est dans les Pensées qu'une petite tache insignifiante, qui n'atteint pas la merveilleuse beauté du fond. La

---

[1] See the preface to Mr. Long's admirable translation. The quotations from the *Meditations* in this essay are given partly in Mr. Long's words.

science pourrait détruire Dieu et l'âme, que le livre des
Pensées resterait jeune encore de vie et de vérité.   La
religion de Marc-Aurèle, comme le fut par moments celle
de Jésus, est la religion absolue, celle qui résulte du
simple fait d'une haute conscience morale placée en face
de l'univers.   Elle n'est ni d'une race ni d'un pays.
Aucune révolution, aucun progrès, aucune découverte ne
pourront la changer."

What then, we may ask, and how attained to,
was the wisdom which is thus highly praised?
How came it that a man of little original power,
in an age of rhetoric and commonplace, was able
to rise to the height of so great an argument, and
to make of his most secret ponderings the religious
manual of a far-distant world?   This question can
scarcely be answered without a few preliminary reflections on the historical development of religion at
Rome.

Among all the civilised religions of antiquity
the Roman might well seem the least congenial
either to the beliefs or to the emotions of modern
times.   From the very first it bears all the marks
of a political origin.   When the antiquarian Varro
treats first of the state and then of the gods, " because in order that gods may be established states
must first exist," he is but retracing faithfully the
real genesis of the cult of Rome.   Composed of
elements borrowed from various quarters, it dealt
with all in a legal, external, unimaginative spirit.

The divination and ghost-religion, which it drew from the Etruscans and other primitive sources, survived in the state-augury and in the domestic worship of the Lares, only in a formal and half-hearted way. The nature-religion, which came from the Aryan forefathers of Rome, grew frigid indeed when it was imprisoned in the *Indigitamenta*, or Official Handy-book of the Gods. It is not to Rome, though it may often be to Italy, that the anthropologist must look for instances of those quaint rites which form in many countries the oldest existing links between civilised and primitive conceptions of the operations of an unseen Power. It is not from Rome that the poet must hope for fresh developments of those exquisite and unconscious allegories, which even in their most hackneyed reproduction still breathe on us the glory of the early world. The most enthusiastic of pagans or neo-pagans could scarcely reverence with much emotion the botanical accuracy of Nodotus, the god of Nodes, and Volutina, the goddess of Petioles, nor tremble before the terrors of Spiniensis and Robigus, the austere Powers of Blight and Brambles, nor eagerly implore the favour of Stercutius and Sterquilinus, the beneficent deities of Manure.[1]

This shadowy system of divinities is a mere

---

[1] Of some of these Powers it is hard to say whether they are to be considered as celestial or the reverse. Such are Carnea, the Goddess of Embonpoint, and Genius Portorii Publici, the Angel of Indirect Taxation.

elaboration of the primitive notion that religion consists in getting whatever can be got from the gods, and that this must be done by asking the right personages in the proper terms. The boast of historian or poet that the old Romans were "most religious mortals," or that they "surpassed in piety the gods themselves," refers entirely to punctuality of outward observance, considered as a definite *quid pro quo* for the good things desired. It is not hard to be "more pious than the gods" if piety on our part consists in asking decorously for what we want, and piety on their part in immediately granting it.

It is plain that it was not in this direction that the Romans found a vent for the reverence and the self-devotion in which their character was assuredly not deficient. Their true worship, their true piety, were reserved for a more concrete, though still a vast ideal. As has been often said, the religion of the Romans was Rome. Her true saints were her patriots, Curtius and Scævola, Horatius, Regulus, Cato. Her "heaven-descended maxim" was not γνῶθι σεαυτὸν, but *Delenda est Carthago*. But a concrete idea must necessarily lose in fixedness what it gains in actuality. As Rome became the Roman Empire the temper of her religion must needs change with the fortunes of its object. While the fates of the city yet hung in the balance the very thought of her had been enough to make *Roman* for all ages a synonym for *heroic* virtue.   But when a heterogeneous world-wide empire seemed to derive its unity from the Emperor's personality alone, men felt that the object of so many deeds of piety had disappeared through their very success.   Devotion to Rome was transformed into the worship of Cæsar, and the one strain of vital religion which had run through the Commonwealth was stiffened like all the rest into a dead official routine.

Something better than this was needed for cultivated and serious men.   To take one instance only, what was the Emperor himself to worship?   It might be very well for obsequious provinces to erect statues to the *Indulgentia Cæsaris*.   But Cæsar himself could hardly be expected to adore his own Good-humour.   In epochs like these, when a national religion has lost its validity in thoughtful minds, and the nation is pausing, as it were, for further light, there is a fair field for all comers. There is an opportunity for those who wish either to eliminate the religious instinct, or to distort it, or to rationalise it, or to vivify; for the secularist and the charlatan, for the philosopher and the prophet.   In Rome there was assuredly no lack of negation and indifference, of superstition and its inseparable fraud.   But two streams of higher tendency rushed into the spiritual vacuum, two currents which represented, broadly speaking, the main religious and the main ethical tradition of mankind. The first of these, which we must pass by for the present, had its origin in the legendary Pythagoras and the remoter East. The second took the form of a generalised and simplified Stoicism.

Stoicism, of course, was no new thing in Rome. It had come in with Greek culture at the time of the Punic wars; it had commended itself by its proud precision to Roman habits of thought and life; it had been welcomed as a support for the state religion, a method of allegorising Olympus which yet might be accounted orthodox. The names of Cato and Brutus maintained the Stoic tradition through the death-throes of the Republic. But the stern independence of the Porch was not invoked to aid in the ceremonial revival with which Augustus would fain have renewed the old Roman virtue. It is among the horrors of Nero's reign that we find Stoicism taking its place as a main spiritual support of men. But as it becomes more efficacious it becomes also less distinctive. In Seneca, in Epictetus, most of all in Marcus himself, we see it gradually discarding its paradoxes, its controversies, its character as a specialised philosophical sect. We hear less of its logic, its cosmogony, its portrait of the ideal Sage. It insists rather on what may be termed the catholic verities of all philosophers, on the sole importance of virtue,

the spiritual oneness of the universe, the brotherhood of men. From every point of view this latter
Stoicism afforded unusual advantages to the soul
which aimed at wisdom and virtue. It was a philosophy; but by dint of time and trial it had run
itself clear of the extravagance and unreality of the
schools. It was a reform; but its attitude towards
the established religion was at once friendly and
independent, so that it was neither cramped by
deference nor embittered by reaction. Its doctrines
were old and true; yet it had about it a certain
freshness as being in fact the first free and medi-
tative outlook on the universe to which the Roman
people had attained. And, more than all, it had
ready to its hand a large remainder of the most
famous store of self-devotedness that the world has
seen. Stoicism was the heir of the old Roman
virtue; happy is the philosophy which can support
its own larger creed on the instincts of duty inherited from many a generation of narrow upright-
ness, of unquestioned law.

But the opportunity for the very flower of Stoic
excellence was due to the caprice of a great amateur.
Hadrian admired both beauty and virtue; his choice
of Antinous and of Marcus gave to the future world
the standard of the sculptor and the standard of
the moralist; the completest types of physical and
moral perfection which Roman history has handed
down. And yet among the names of his bene-

factors with which the scrupulous gratitude of
Marcus has opened his self-communings, the name
Hadrianus does not occur. The boy thus raised
to empire has passed by Hadrian, who gave him
all the kingdoms of the world and the glory of
them, for Severus, who taught him to disdain them
all.

Among all the *Meditations* none is at once more
simple and more original than this exordium of
thanksgiving. It is the single-hearted utterance of
a soul which knows neither desire nor pride, which
considers nothing as gain in her life's journey except the love of those souls who have loved her,—
the memory of those who have fortified her by the
spectacle and communication of virtue.

The thoughts that follow on this prelude are by
no means of an exclusively Stoic type. They are
both more emotional and more agnostic than would
have satisfied Chrysippus or Zeno. They are not
conceived in that tone of certainty and conviction
in which men lecture or preach, but with those sad
reserves, those varying moods of hope and despondency, which are natural to a man's secret ponderings
on the riddle of the world. Even the fundamental
Stoic belief in God and Providence is not beyond
question in Marcus' eyes. The passages where he
repeats the alternative " either gods or atoms " are
too strongly expressed to allow us to think that the
antithesis is only a trick of style.

"Either confusion and entanglement and scattering again : or unity, order, providence. If the first case be, why do I wish to live amid the clashings of chance and chaos? or care for aught else but to become earth myself at last? and why am I disturbed, since this dispersion will come whatever I do? but if the latter case be the true one, I reverence and stand firm, and trust in him who rules.

"Thus wags the world, up and down, from age to age. And either the universal mind determines each event; and if so, accept then that which it determines; or it has ordered once for all, and the rest follows in sequence; or indivisible elements are the origin of all things. In a word, if there be a god, then all is well; if all things go at random, act not at random thou."

And along with this speculative openness, so much more sympathetic to the modern reader than the rhetoric of Seneca or even the lofty dogmatism of Epictetus, there is a total absence of the Stoic pride. His self-reverence is of that truest kind which is based on a man's conception not of what he is, but of what he ought to be.

"Men cannot admire the sharpness of thy wits. Be it so; but many other things there are of which thou canst not say, I was not formed for them. Show those things which are wholly in thy power to show : sincerity, dignity, laboriousness, self-denial, contentment, frugality, kindliness, frankness, simplicity, seriousness, magnanimity. Seest thou not how many things there are in which, with no excuse of natural incapacity, thou voluntarily fallest short? or art thou compelled by defect of nature

to murmur and be stingy and flatter and complain of
thy poor body, and cajole and boast, and disquiet thyself in vain? No, by the gods! but of all these things
thou mightest have been rid long ago. Nay, if indeed
thou be somewhat slow and dull of comprehension, thou
must exert thyself about this too, and not neglect it nor
be contented with thy dulness."

Words like these, perhaps, exalt human nature
in our eyes quite as highly as if we had heard Marcus insisting, like some others of his school, that
"the sage is as useful to Zeus as Zeus to him," or
that "courage is more creditable to sages than it is
to gods, since gods have it by nature, but sages by
practice."

And having thus overheard his self-communings,
with what a sense of soundness and reality do we
turn to the steady fervour of his constantly repeated
ideal!

"Let the god within thee be the guardian of a living
being, masculine, adult, political, and a Roman, and a
ruler; who has taken up his post in life as one that
awaits with readiness the signal that shall summon him
away. . . . And such a man, who delays no longer to
strive to be in the number of the best, is as a priest and
servant of the gods, obeying that god who is in himself
enshrined, who renders him unsoiled of pleasure, un-
harmed by any pain, untouched by insult, feeling no
wrong, a wrestler in the noblest struggle, which is, that
by no passion he may be overthrown; dyed to the depth
in justice, and with his whole heart welcoming whatsoever cometh to him and is ordained."

The ideal is sketched on Stoic lines, but the writer's temperament is not cast in the old Stoic mould. He reminds us rather of modern sensitiveness, in his shrinking from the presence of coarse and selfish persons, and in his desire, obvious enough but constantly checked, for the sympathy and approbation of those with whom he lived. The self-sufficing aspect of Stoicism has in him lost all its exclusiveness; it is represented only by the resolute recurrence to conscience as the one support against the buffets of the world.

"I do my duty; other things trouble me not; for either they are things without life, or things without reason, or things that have wandered and know not the way."

And thus, while all the dealings of Marcus with his fellow-men are summed up in the two endeavours —to imitate their virtues, and to amend, or at least patiently to endure, their defects—it is pretty plain which of these two efforts was most frequently needed. His fragmentary thoughts present us with a long series of struggles to rise from the mood of disgust and depression into the mood of serene benevolence, by dwelling strongly on a few guiding lines of self-admonition.

"Begin the morning by saying to thyself: I shall meet with the busybody, the ungrateful, arrogant, deceitful, envious, unsocial. All these things happen to them by reason of their ignorance of what is good and evil. But I who have seen the nature of the good that it is

beautiful, and of the bad that it is ugly, and the nature
of him who sins, that it is akin to mine, and partici-
pates in the same divinity, I can neither be injured by
any of them, for no man can fix a foulness on me;
nor can I be angry nor hate my brother."

There is reason, indeed, to fear that Marcus loved
his enemies too well; that he was too much given
to blessing those that cursed him. It is to him,
rather than to any Christian potentate, that we must
look for an example of the dangers of applying the
gospel maxims too unreservedly to the business of
the turbid world. For indeed the practical danger
lies not in the overt adoption of those counsels of
an ideal mildness and mercy, but even in the mere
attainment of a temper so calm and lofty that the
promptings of vanity or anger are felt no more.
The task of curbing and punishing other men, of
humiliating their arrogance, exposing their falsity,
upbraiding their sloth, is in itself so distasteful, when
there is no personal rivalry or resentment to prompt
it, that it is sure to be performed too gently, or
neglected for more congenial duties. Avidius Cassius, burning his disorderly soldiers alive to gain
himself a reputation for vigour, was more compre-
hensible to the mass of men, more immediately efficacious, than Marcus representing to the selfish and
wayward Commodus "that even bees did not act in
such a manner, nor any of those creatures which live
in troops."

But the very incongruity between the duties which Marcus was called on to perform and the spirit which he brought to their performance, the fate which made him by nature a sage and a saint, by profession a ruler and a warrior, all this gave to his character a dignity and a completeness which it could scarcely otherwise have attained. The master of the world more than other men might feel himself bound to "live as on a mountain;" he whose look was life or death to millions might best set the example of the single-heartedness which need hide the thought of no waking moment from any one's knowledge,—till a man's eyes should reveal all that passed within him, "even as there is no veil upon a star." The Stoic philosophy which required that the sage should be indifferent to worldly goods found its crowning exemplar in a sage who possessed them all.

And, indeed, in the case of Marcus the difficulty was not to disdain the things of earth, but to care for them enough. The touch of Cynic crudity with which he analyses such things as men desire, reminds us sometimes of those scornful pictures of secular life which have been penned in the cloister. For that indifference to transitory things which has often made the religious fanatic the worst of citizens is not the danger of the fanatic alone. It is a part also of the melancholy of the magnanimous; of the mood when the "joy and gladness" which the Stoics promised to their sage die down in the midst of "such darkness and dirt," as Marcus calls it, "that it is hard to imagine what there is which is worthy to be prized highly, or seriously pursued."

Nay, it seems to him that even if, in Plato's phrase, he could become "the spectator of all time and of all existence," there would be nothing in the sight to stir the exultation, to change the solitude of the sage. The universe is full of living creatures, but there is none of them whose existence is so glorious and blessed that by itself it can justify all other Being; the worlds are destroyed and re-created with an endless renewal, but they are tending to no world more pure than themselves; they are not even, as in Hindoo myth, ripening in a secular expectancy till Buddha come; they are but repeating the same littlenesses from the depth to the height of heaven, and reiterating throughout all eternity the fears and follies of a day.

"If thou wert lifted on high and didst behold the manifold fates of men; and didst discern at once all creatures that dwell round about him, in the ether and the air; then howso oft thou thus wert raised on high, these same things thou shouldst ever see, all things alike, and all things perishing. And where is, then, the glory?"

Men who look out on the world with a gaze thus disenchanted are apt to wrap themselves in a cynical indifference or in a pessimistic despair. But character is stronger than creed; and Marcus carries

into the midst of the saddest surroundings his
nature's imperious craving to reverence and to love.
He feels, indeed, that the one joy which could have
attached him to the world is wholly wanting to him.

"This is the only thing, if anything there be, which
could have drawn thee backwards and held thee still in
life, if it had been granted thee to live with men of like
principles with thyself.   But now thou seest how great
a pain there is in the discordance of thy life with other
men's, so that thou sayest: Come quick, O death! lest
perchance I too should forget myself."

Nor can he take comfort from any steadfast hope
of future fellowship with kindred souls.

"How can it be that the gods, having ordered all
things rightly and with good-will towards men, have
overlooked this thing alone: that some men, virtuous
indeed, who have as it were made many a covenant with
heaven, and through holy deeds and worship have had
closest communion with the divine, that these men, when
once they are dead, should not live again, but be extinguished for ever?   Yet if this be so, be sure that if it
ought to have been otherwise the gods would have done
it.   For were it just, it would also be possible; were it
according to nature, nature would have had it so."

For thus he believes without proof and without
argument that all is for the best; that everything
which happens is for the advantage of every con-
stituent life in nature, since everything is for the
advantage of the whole.   He will not entertain the
idea that the Powers above him may be not all-

powerful; or the Wisdom which rules the universe less than all-wise. And this optimism comes from no natural buoyancy of temper. There is scarcely a trace in the *Meditations* of any mood of careless joy. He never rises beyond the august contentment of the man who accepts his fate.

"All things are harmonious to me which are harmonious to thee, O Universe. Nothing for me is too early nor too late which is in due time for thee. All is fruit to me which thy seasons, O Nature, bear. From thee are all things, and in thee all, and all return to thee. The poet says, 'Dear city of Cecrops;' shall I not say, 'Dear city of God?'"

There have been many who, with no more belief than Marcus in a personal immortality, have striven, like him, to accept willingly the world in which they found themselves placed. But sometimes they have marred the dignity of their position by attempting too eagerly to find a reason for gladness; they have dwelt with exultation upon a terrene future for our race from which Marcus would still have turned and asked, "Where, then, is the glory?" It would have seemed to him that a triumphant tone like this can only come from the soilure of philosophy with something of the modern spirit of industrial materialism and facile enjoyment; he would have preferred that his own sereneness should be less near to complacency than to resignation; he would still have chosen the temper of that saintly Stoic, whose rude, strong verses break in with so stern a piety among the fragments of philosophic Greece :—

> "Lead, lead Cleanthes, Zeus and holy Fate,
> Where'er ye place my post, to serve or wait:
> Willing I follow ; were it not my will,
> A baffled rebel I must follow still."

These, however, are differences only of tone and temper overlying what forms in reality a vast body of practical agreement. For the scheme of thought and belief which has thus been briefly sketched is not only in itself a noble and a just one. It is a kind of common creed of wise men, from which all other views may well seem mere deflections on the side of an unwarranted credulity or of an exaggerated despair. Here, it may be not unreasonably urged, is the moral backbone of all universal religions ; and as civilisation has advanced, the practical creed of all parties, whatever their speculative pretensions, has approximated ever more nearly to these plain principles and uncertain hopes.

This view of the tendency of religious progress is undoubtedly the simplest and most plausible which history presents to the philosopher who is not himself pledged to the defence of any one form of what is termed supernatural belief. But it has to contend with grave difficulties of historical fact ; and among these difficulties the age of the Antonines presents one of the most considerable. Never had the ground been cleared on so large a scale for pure philosophy; never was there so little external pressure exerted in favour of any traditional faith. The persecutions of the Christians were undertaken on political and moral, rather than on theological grounds; they were the expression of the feeling with which a modern State might regard a set of men who were at once Mormons and Nihilists—refusing the legal tokens of respect to constituted authorities, while suspected of indulging in low immorality at the bidding of an ignorant superstition. And yet the result of this age of tolerance and enlightenment was the gradual recrudescence, among the cultivated as well as the ignorant, of the belief in a perceptible interaction of the seen and the unseen world, culminating at last in the very form of that belief which had shown itself most resolute, most thorough-going, and most intractable.

For the triumph of Christianity in the Roman Empire must not be looked upon as an anomalous or an isolated phenomenon. It was rather the triumph along the whole line, though (as is usual in great triumphs) in an unlooked-for fashion, of a current of tendency which had coexisted obscurely with State-religion, patriotism, and philosophy, almost from the first beginnings of the city. The anomaly, if there were one, consisted in the fact that the hints and elements of this new power, which was destined to be the second life of Rome, were to be found, not in the time-honoured ordinances of her Senate, or the sober wisdom of her schools, but in the fanaticism of ignorant enthusiasts, in the dreams of a mystic poet, in the alleged, but derided, experiences of a few eccentric philosophers. The introduction of Christianity at Rome was the work not only of Peter and Paul, but of Virgil and Varro.

For amidst the various creeds and philosophies, by aid of which men have ordered their life on earth, the most persistent and fundamental line of division is surely this :—The question whether that life is to be ordered by rules drawn from its own experience alone, or whether there are indications which may justly modify our conduct or expectations by some influx of inspiration, or some phenomena testifying to the existence of an unseen world, or to our continued life after the body's decay? The instincts which prompt to this latter view found, as has been already implied, but little sustenance in the established cult of Rome. They were forced to satisfy themselves in a fitful and irregular fashion by Greek and Oriental modes of religious excitement. What sense of elevation or reality may have been present to the partakers in these alien enthusiasms we are not now able to say. The worships of Bacchus and Cybele have been described to us by historians of the same conservative temper as those who afterwards made " an execrable superstition " of the worship of Christ.

Some scattered indications seem to imply a substratum of religious emotion, or of theurgic experiment, more extensive than the ordinary authorities have cared to record.   The proud and gay Catullus rises to his masterpiece in the description of that alternation of reckless fanaticism and sick recoil which formed throughout the so-called Ages of Faith the standing tragedy of the cloister.   More startling still is the story which shows us a group of the greatest personages of Rome in the last century before Christ, Nigidius Figulus, Appius Claudius, Publius Vatinius, Marcus Varro, subjected to police supervision on account of their alleged practice of summoning into visible presence the spirits of the dead.   "The whole system," says Professor Mommsen, "obtained its consecration—political, religious, and national—from the name of Pythagoras, the ultra-conservative statesman, whose supreme principle was 'to promote order and to check disorder,' the miracle-worker and necromancer, the primeval sage who was a native of Italy, who was interwoven even with the legendary history of Rome, and whose statue was to be seen in the Roman Forum."   This story might seem an isolated one but for one remarkable literary parallel.   In Virgil—perhaps the only Roman writer who possessed what would now be termed religious originality—we observe the co-existence of three separate lines of religious thought. There is the conservatism which loses no opportunity of enforcing the traditional worships of Rome, in

accordance at once with the poet's own temper of
mind, and with the plan of Augustus' ethical reforms.
There is the new fusion of the worship of Rome
with the worship of the Emperor—the only symbol
of spiritual unity between remote provincials and
the imperial city. But finally, in the central passage
of his greatest poem, we come on a Pythagorean
creed, expressed, indeed, with some confusion and
hesitancy, but with earnest conviction and power,
and forming, as the well-known fragment of correspondence plainly implies, the dominant pre-occupation of the poet's later life.

Such a scheme, indeed, as the Pythagorean, with
its insistence on a personal immortality, and its
moral retribution adjusted by means of successive
existences with a greater nicety than has been employed by any other creed—such a scheme, if once
established, might have satisfied the spiritual needs of
the Roman world more profoundly and permanently
than either the worship of Jove or the worship of
Cæsar. But it was not established. The reasoning,
or the evidence, which had impressed Virgil, or the
group of philosophers, was not set forth before the
mass of men; those instincts which we should now
term specifically religious remained unguided; and
during the next three centuries we observe the love
of the marvellous and the supernatural dissociating
itself more and more from any ethical dogma. There
are, no doubt, remarkable instances in these centuries

of an almost modern spirit of piety associated (as for instance in Apuleius) with the most bizarre religious vagaries. But on the whole the two worships which, until the triumph of Christianity, seemed most likely to overrun the civilised world were the worship of Mithra and the worship of Serapis. Now the name of Mithra can hardly be connected with moral conceptions of any kind. And the nearest that we can get to the character of Serapis is the fact that he was by many persons considered to be identical either with the principle of good or with the principle of evil.

Among these confused and one-sided faiths Christianity had an unique superiority. It was the only formulated and intelligible creed which united the two elements most necessary for a widely-received religion, namely, a lofty moral code, and the attestation of some actual intercourse between the visible and the invisible worlds.

It was not the morality of the Gospels alone which exercised the attractive force. Still less was it the speculations of Pauline theology, the high conceptions which a later age hardened into so immutable a system. It was the fact that this lofty teaching was based on beliefs which almost all men held already; that exhortations, nobler than those of Plutarch or Marcus, were supported by marvels better attested than those of Alexander of Abonoteichos, or Apollonius of Tyana. In a thousand ways, and by a thousand channels, the old faiths

melted into the new.   It was not only that such
apologists as Justin and Minucius Felix were fond
of showing that Christianity was, as it were, the
crown of philosophy, the consummation of Platonic
truth.   More important was the fact that the rank
and file of Christian converts looked on the universe
with the same eyes as the heathens around them.
All that they asked of these was to believe that the
dimly-realised deities, whom the heathens regarded
rather with fear than love, were in reality powers of
evil; while above the Oriental additions so often made
to their Pantheon was to be superposed one ultimate
divinity, alone beneficent, and alone to be adored.

The hierarchy of an unseen universe must needs
be a somewhat shadowy and arbitrary thing.   To
those, indeed, whose imagination is already exercised
on such matters a new scheme of the celestial powers
may come with an acceptable sense of increasing
insight into the deep things of God.   But in one
who, like Marcus, has learnt to believe that in such
matters the truest wisdom is to recognise that we
cannot know, in him a scheme like the Christian
is apt to inspire incredulity by its very promise of
completeness,—suspicion by the very nature of the
evidence which is alleged in its support.

Neither the Stoic school in general, indeed, nor
Marcus himself, were clear of all superstitious tendency.   The early masters of the sect had pushed
their doctrine of the solidarity of all things to the

point of anticipating that the liver of a particular bullock, itself selected from among its fellows by some mysterious fitness of things, might reasonably give an indication of the result of an impending battle. When it was urged that on this principle everything might be expected to be indicative of everything else, the Stoics answered that so it was, but that only when such indications lay in the liver could we understand them aright. When asked how we came to understand them when thus located, the Stoic doctors seem to have made no sufficient reply. We need not suppose that Marcus participated in absurdities like these. He himself makes no assertion of this hazardous kind, except only that remedies for his ailments " have been shown to him in dreams." And this is not insisted on in detail; it rather forms part of that habitual feeling or impression which, if indeed it be superstitious, is yet a superstition from which no devout mind, perhaps, was ever wholly free; namely, that he is the object of a special care and benevolence proceeding from some holy power. Such a feeling implies no belief either in merit or in privilege beyond that of other men; but just as the man who is strongly willing, though it be proved to him that his choice is determined by his antecedents, must yet feel assured that he can deflect its issue this way or that, even so a man, the habit of whose soul is worship, cannot but see at least a reflection of his own virtue in the arch of heaven, and bathe his spirit in the mirage projected from the well-spring of its own love.

For such an instinct, for all the highest instincts of his heart, Marcus would no doubt have found in Christianity a new and full satisfaction. The question, however, whether he ought to have become a Christian is not worth serious discussion. In the then state of belief in the Roman world it would have been as impossible for a Roman Emperor to become a Christian as it would be at the present day for a Czar of Russia to become a Buddhist. Some Christian apologists complain that Marcus was not converted by the miracle of the " Thundering Legion." They forget that though some obscure persons may have ascribed that happy occurrence to Christian prayers, the Emperor was assured on much higher authority that he had performed the miracle himself. Marcus, indeed, would assuredly not have insisted on his own divinity. He would not have been deterred by any Stoic exclusiveness from incorporating in his scheme of belief, already infiltrated with Platonic thought, such elements as those apologists who start from St. Paul's speech at Athens would have urged him to introduce. But an acceptance of the new faith involved much more than this. It involved tenets which might well seem to be a mere reversion to the world-old superstitions and sorceries of barbarous tribes. Such alleged phenomena as those of possession, inspiration, healing by imposition of hands, luminous appearances, modification and movement of material objects, formed, not, as some later apologists would have it, a mere accidental admixture, but an essential and loudly-asserted element in the new religion. The apparition of its Founder after death was its very *raison d'être* and triumphant demonstration. The Christian advocate may say indeed with reason, that phenomena such as these, however suspicious the associations which they might invoke, however primitive the stratum of belief to which they might seem at first to degrade the disciple, should nevertheless have been examined afresh on their own evidence, and would have been found to be supported by a consensus of testimony which has since then overcome the world. Addressed to an age in which Reason was supreme, such arguments might have carried convincing weight. But mankind had certainly not reached a point in the age of the Antonines,—if indeed we have reached it yet,—at which the recollections of barbarism were cast into so remote a background that the leaders of civilised thought could lightly reopen questions the closing of which might seem to have marked a clear advance along the path of enlightenment. It is true, indeed, that the path of enlightenment is not a royal road but a labyrinth; and that those who have marched too unhesitatingly in one direction have generally been obliged to retrace their steps, to unravel some forgotten clue, to explore some turning which they had already passed by.　But the practical rulers of men must not take the paths which seem to point backwards until they hear in front of them the call of those who have chosen that less inviting way.

An emperor who had " learnt from Diognetus not to give credit to what is said by miracle-workers and jugglers about incantations and the driving away of demons and such things," might well feel that so much as to inquire into the Gospel stories would be a blasphemy against his philosophic creed.　Even the heroism of Christian martyrdom left him cold.　In words which have become proverbial as a wise man's mistake, he stigmatises the Christian contempt of death as " sheer party spirit."　And yet—it is an old thought, but it is impossible not to recur to it once more—what might he not have learnt from these despised sectaries ! the melancholy Emperor from Potheinus and Blandina, smiling on the rack !

Of the Christian virtues, it was not *faith* which was lacking to him.　His faith indeed was not that bastard faith of theologians, which is nothing more than a willingness to assent to historical propositions on insufficient evidence.　But it was faith such as Christ demanded of His disciples, the steadfastness of the soul in clinging, spite of doubts, of difficulties, even of despair, to whatever she has known of best ; the resolution to stand or fall by the noblest hypothesis.　To Marcus the alternative of " gods or

atoms "—of a universe ruled either by blind chance
or by an intelligent Providence—was ever present
and ever unsolved; but in action he ignored that
dark possibility, and lived as a member of a sacred
cosmos, and co-operant with ordering gods.

Again, it might seem unjust to say that he was
wanting in love. No one has expressed with more
conviction the interdependence and kinship of men.

"We are made to work together, like feet, like hands,
like eyelids, like the rows of the upper and lower teeth."
"It is peculiar to man to love even those who do wrong;
and thou wilt love them if, when they err, thou bethink
thee that they are to thee near akin." "Men exist for
the sake of one another; teach them then, or bear with
them." "When men blame thee, or hate thee, or revile
thee, pass inward to their souls; see what they are.
Thou wilt see that thou needst not trouble thyself as to
what such men think of thee. And thou must be kindly
affectioned to them; for by nature they are friends;
and the gods, too, help and answer them in many ways."
"Love men, and love them from the heart." "'Earth
loves the shower,' and 'sacred æther loves;' and the
whole universe loves the making of that which is to be.
I say then to the universe: Even I, too, love as thou."

And yet about the love of a John, a Paul, a
Peter, there is the ring of a note which is missing
here. Stoic love is but an injunction of reason and
a means to virtue; Christian love is the open secret
of the universe, and in itself the end of all. In all
that wisdom can teach herein, Stoic and Christian

are at one. They both know that if a man would save his life he must lose it; that the disappearance of all selfish aims or pleasures in the universal life is the only pathway to peace. All religions that are worth the name have felt the need of this inward change; the difference lies rather in the light under which they regard it. To the Stoic in the West, as to the Buddhist in the East, it presented itself as a renunciation which became a deliverance, a tranquillity which passed into an annihilation. The Christian, too, recognised in the renunciation of the world a deliverance from its evil. But his spirit in those early days was occupied less with what he was resigning than with what he gained; the love of Christ constrained him; he died to self to find, even here on earth, that he had passed not into nothingness, but into heaven. In his eyes the Stoic doctrine was not false, but partly rudimentary and partly needless. His only objection, if objection it could be called, to the Stoic manner of facing the reality of the universe, was that the reality of the universe was so infinitely better than the Stoic supposed.

If, then, the Stoic love beside the Christian was "as moonlight unto sunlight, and as water unto wine," it was not only because the Stoic philosophy prescribed the curbing and checking of those natural emotions which Christianity at once guided and intensified by her new ideal. It was because the love

of Christ which the Christian felt was not a labori-
ous duty, but a self-renewing, self-intensifying force ;
a feeling offered as to one who for ever responded
to it, as to one whose triumphant immortality had
brought his disciples' immortality to light.

So completely had the appearance of Jesus to
the faithful after his apparent death altered in
their eyes the aspect of the world.   So decisive
was the settlement of the old alternative, " Either
Providence or atoms," which was effected by the
firm conviction of a single spirit's beneficent return
along that silent and shadowy way.   So powerful a
reinforcement to Faith and Love was afforded by
the third of the Christian trinity of virtues—by the
grace of Hope.

But we are treading here on controverted ground.
It is not only that this great prospect has not yet
taken its place among admitted certainties ; that
the hope and resurrection of the dead are still called
in question.   Much more than this; the most advanced school of modern moralists tends rather to
deny that "a sure and certain hope" in this matter
is to be desired at all.   Virtue, it is alleged, must
needs lose her disinterestedness if the solution of
the great problem were opened to her gaze.

"Pour nous," says M. Renan, who draws this moral
especially from the noble disinterestedness of Marcus
himself: "pour nous, on nous annoncerait un argument
péremptoire en ce genre, que nous ferions comme Saint

Louis, quand on lui parla de l'hostie miraculeuse ; nous refuserions d'aller voir. Qu'avons nous besoin de ces preuves brutales, qui n'ont d'application que dans l'ordre grossier des faits, et qui gêneraient notre liberté ?"

This seems a strong argument; and if it be accepted it is practically decisive of the question at issue,—I do not say only between Stoicism and Christianity, but between all those systems which do not seek, and those which do seek, a spiritual communion for man external to his own soul, a spiritual continuance external to his own body. If a proof of a beneficent Providence or of a future life be a thing to be deprecated, it will be indiscreet, or even immoral, to inquire whether such proof has been, or can be, obtained. The world must stand with Marcus; and there will be no extravagance in M. Renan's estimate of the Stoic morality as a sounder and more permanent system than that of Jesus Himself.

But generalisations like this demand a close examination. Is the antithesis between interested and disinterested virtue a clear and fundamental one for all stages of spiritual progress? Or may we not find that the conditions of the experiment vary, as it were, as virtue passes through different temperatures; that our formula gives a positive result at one point, a negative at another, and becomes altogether unmeaning at a third?

It will be allowed, in the first place, that for an

indefinite time to come, and until the mass of mankind has advanced much higher above the savage level than is as yet the case, it will be premature to be too fastidious as to the beliefs which prompt them to virtue. The first object is to give them habits of self-restraint and well-doing, and we may be well content if their crude notions of an unseen Power are such as to reinforce the somewhat obscure indications which life on earth at present affords that honesty and truth and mercy bring a real reward to men. But let us pass on to the extreme hypothesis on which the repudiation of any spiritual help for man outside himself must ultimately rest. Let us suppose that man's impulses have become harmonised with his environment; that his tendency to anger has been minimised by long-standing gentleness; his tendency to covetousness by diffused well-being; his tendency to sensuality by the increased preponderance of his intellectual nature. How will the test of his disinterestedness operate then? Why, it will be no more possible then for a sane man to be deliberately wicked than it is possible now for a civilised man to be deliberately filthy in his personal habits. We do not wish now that it were uncertain whether filth were unhealthy in order that we might be the more meritorious in preferring to be clean. And whether our remote descendants have become convinced of the reality of a future life or no, it will assuredly never occur to them that, without it, there might be a question whether virtue was a remunerative object of pursuit. Lapses from virtue there may still be in plenty; but inherited instinct will have made it inconceivable that a man should voluntarily be what Marcus calls a "boil or imposthume upon the universe," an island of selfishness in the mid-sea of sympathetic joy.

It is true, indeed, that in the present age, and for certain individuals, that choice of which M. Renan speaks has a terrible, a priceless reality. Many a living memory records some crisis when one who had rejected as unproved the traditional sanctions was forced to face the question whether his virtue had any sanction which still could stand; some night when the foundations of the soul's deep were broken up, and she asked herself why she still should cleave to the law of other men rather than to some kindlier monition of her own :—

> "Doch alles was dazu mich trieb,
> Gott, war so gut! ach, war so lieb!"

To be the conqueror in such a contest is the characteristic privilege of a time of transition like our own. But it is not the only, nor even the highest conceivable, form of virtue. It is an incident in the moral life of the individual; its possibility may be but an incident in the moral life of the race. It is but driving the enemy off the ground

on which we wish to build our temple; there
may be far greater trials of strength, endurance,
courage, before we have raised its dome in air.

For after all it is only in the lower stages of
ethical progress that to see the right is easy and to
decide on doing it is hard. The time comes when
it is not so much conviction of the desirability of
virtue that is needed, as enlightenment to perceive
where virtue's upward pathway lies; not so much
the direction of the will which needs to be controlled, as its force and energy which need to be
ever vivified and renewed. It is then that the
moralist must needs welcome any influence, if such
there be, which can pour into man's narrow vessel
some overflowing of an infinite Power. It is then,
too, that he will learn to perceive that the promise
of a future existence might well be a source of
potent stimulus rather than of enervating peace.
For if we are to judge of the reward of virtue
hereafter by the rewards which we see her achieving here, it is manifest that the only reward which
always attends her is herself; that the only prize
which is infallibly gained by performing one duty
well is the power of performing yet another; the
only recompense for an exalted self-forgetfulness is
that a man forgets himself always more. Or rather,
the only other reward ·is one whose sweetness also
is scarcely realisable till it is attained; it is the
love of kindred souls; but a love which recedes

ever farther from the flatteries and indulgences which most men desire, and tends rather to become the intimate comradeship of spirits that strive towards the same goal.

Why then should those who would imagine an eternal reward for virtue imagine her as eternally rewarded in any other way? And what need there be in a spiritual law like this to relax any soul's exertion, to encourage any low content? By an unfailing physical law we know that the athlete attains through painful effort that alacrity and soundness which are the health of the body. And if there were an unfailing spiritual law by which the philosopher might attain, and ever attain increasingly, through strenuous virtue, that energy and self-devotedness which are the health of the soul, would there be anything in the one law or in the other to encourage either the physical or the spiritual voluptuary—the self-indulgence either of the banquet-hall or of the cloister? There would be no need to test men by throwing an artificial uncertainty round the operation of such laws as these; it would be enough if they could desire what was offered to them; the ideal would become the probation.

To some minds reflections like these, rather than like M. Renan's, will be suggested by the story of Marcus, of his almost unmingled sadness, his almost stainless virtue. All will join, indeed, in admiration for a life so free from every unworthy, every dubious incitement to well-doing. But on comparing this life with the lives of men for whom the great French critic's sympathy is so much less—such men, for instance, as St. Paul—we may surely feel that if the universe be in reality so much better than Marcus supposed, it would have done him good, not harm, to have known it; that it would have kindled his wisdom to a fervent glow, such as the world can hardly hope to see, till, if ever it be so, the dicta of science and the promises of religion are at one; till saints are necessarily philosophers, and philosophers saints. And yet, whatever inspiring secrets the future may hold, the lover of humanity can never regret that Marcus knew but what he knew. Whatever winds of the spirit may sweep over the sea of souls, the life of Marcus will remain for ever as the normal high-water mark of the unassisted virtue of man. No one has shown more simply or more completely what man at any rate must do and be. No one has ever earned the right to say to himself with a more tranquil assurance—in the words which close the *Meditations*—"Depart thou then contented, for he that releaseth thee is content."

END OF VOL. I.

Printed by R. & R. CLARK, LIMITED, *Edinburgh*.